The Crypto-Capers
in
The Case of the Missing Sock

THE CRYPTO-CAPERS IN

THE CASE OF THE MISSING SOCK

Renée Hand

NORTH STAR PRESS OF ST. CLOUD, INC.
St. Cloud, Minnesota

To Autumn Noel, Isabelle Grace, Sabryn Estelle and
Pierson Jeffrey, you are my inspiration.

Also to my family, Cary, Gabriel and Sheldon, the
heroes of my life.

Cover Art and drawings by Alla Dubrovich
alla.dubrovich@esmail.mcc.edu

ISBN-10: 0-87839-304-8
ISBN-13: 978-0-87839-304-6

Printed in the United States of America.

Published by
North Star Press of St. Cloud, Inc.
P.O. Box 451
St. Cloud, Minnesota 56302
northstarpress.com
info@northstarpress.com

A NOTE TO READERS

In the Crypto-Capers Detective Series, you will run into cryptograms, word scrambles and various other puzzles. You will need to solve these puzzles to bring resolution to the case. If you get stuck, or need extra help, there is an answer key in the back of the book to help you. Each book in the series gets progressively harder. In some cases you will use a given key to fill in the cryptogram and in others you might have to create your own key. Some clues may be given to you in the story to help fill in the cryptogram, and sometimes you will get very little information, in that case you must rely on your own brain power.

A cryptogram is a communication written in code. It is rendered unreadable through the use of what is called a "substitution cipher." What this means is that each letter used in the original message has been substituted for another. For example, A becomes M, G becomes Z, and so forth.

When using a given key, the top row is the alphabet. The bottom row is the alphabet switched around. Like so:

A	B	C	D	E	F	G	H	I	J	K	L	M	N	O	P	Q	R	S	T	U	V	W	X	Y	Z
F	E	B	Y	C	M	N	V	O	L	X	A	K	U	P	Q	I	S	G	D	T	J	Z	R	H	W

When looking at your cryptogram, match each letter from the message with the bottom letter from the key.

When given, for example this cryptogram:

V C A A P

You see the V matches with the H, the C matches with the E. Then you have two A's, which become two L's, and the P at the end becomes an O—H E L L O.

Voila, you have the answer. If your codes message has a number of words, write them down and keep going. What you will end up with is the unscrambled message.

So, let the challenge begin. The game is a foot and the Crypto-Capers love a good mystery.

ODGO KUCL!

Renée Hand

ONE

"FIVE MINUTES! JUST FIVE MORE MINUTES," said Max Holmes quietly as he surveyed the dark room in front of him. This should be the last place to reach, the highest test of his skills. He switched off his flashlight. He faced a rugged stone wall. From somewhere far above him, a crack let in a single, narrow beam of sunshine. It hit about the middle of the wall, barely lighting up a recess, an indention shaped into a rectangle, slightly taller than wide. *A box could fit in there*, Max thought, and he grew just a little nervous. "Did I come here for nothing?" he asked in frustration as he glanced more intently at the wall. "Did I pick the wrong way?" For just a moment, he reviewed his route to this stone box of a room. No, he had made each choice carefully. "This has to be the right place. It has to be here!"

Max walked closer to the wall, analyzing it. He flicked on his flashlight again and played it over each of the four walls. Nothing presented itself to him, except cold hard rock, each wall looking similar, yet different.

Though he knew this had been a constructed space, the room felt very cavelike with its natural-looking stone walls, and yet light still managed to get through from the hole in the rock above him. He glanced at his watch, knowing he had to act soon, that time was running out for him, and refocused his attention on the wall in front of him where the thin, bright beam of light beckoned his attention. After several seconds of deep concentration, Max started to laugh. No, indeed, this was not a natural wall, however, someone had gone to the trouble to make it appear so.

A light gray stripe marked the middle of the wall from floor to ceiling, and it passed right through the indention. This stripe wasn't dark or obvious, looking simply as if the sun had beaten on it brutally—fading it.

"It can't be that simple." Max's words echoed faintly. He swung his backpack from his shoulders and, using his flashlight to explore the contents, took out a small rubber ball that he had found earlier in the tunnels. He also took out a boom-a-rang, which he laid beside the backpack, and, after a moment's thought grabbed the raincoat as well. Max put the raincoat on and walked closer to the wall until he stood a few feet from the indention, tossing the ball back and forth in his hands.

The ground by his feet had an unusually flat surface that did not match with the surrounding rough floor. Glancing up, he saw an identical flat surface on the ceiling. He realized that the two spots lined up perfectly on top of one another. Max then turned his attention to the indentation in the wall. Carefully—one always must be careful where one's fingers were placed if one hoped to retain a full set—Max eased his hand inside the indention. With a delicate touch, he felt several small holes surrounding the bottom flat surface of rock. There was only a two-foot clearance between the top and bottom of the recess. If he timed it just right he could make it. Max studied the geometry of the recess and the smooth ceiling and floor plates that lined up with it. Fishing a piece of chalk from his pocket, he marked an arrow on the wall by his knee. He rechecked his math, then stood up.

As he dropped the chalk back into his pocket, he back pedaled to the opening of the room in the opposite wall, keeping an eye on his chalk mark. He figured he had one shot and one only—and he was nearly out of time. He took a deep breath, held the ball firmly in his hands, then suddenly rushed forward and tossed it gently. He watched as the ball made contact, landing in the middle of the flat surface on the ground. In that moment, the plate sprang upward as if it on coils. This batted the ball upward, and it hit the matching flat surface on the ceiling, causing it to spring as well, tossing the ball across the room.

Max ignored the ball, concentrating instead on what would happen. Without thinking about it, he held his breath. For a few seconds nothing happened, and Max worried that he had made a mistake, but then he heard the loud grinding sound of rock against rock.

The faded strip of rock, which included the indention, was now thrust three feet forward, presenting a thin dividing wall partway into the room with a gap where the indentation was.

This gave Max the opportunity he needed. He began to count to twenty as he reached for his backpack and grabbed the boom-a-rang. When he turned around, he lined himself up, brought his arm back with the boom-a-rang, and waited. At twenty, he saw a piece of paper almost magically appear within the indention. It was then Max threw the boom-a-rang.

The aerodynamic angle of wood twirled and twirled, creating a *whirring* sound in the still air. It spun sometimes so fast that he had a hard time focusing on it. Tensely Max clenched his hands. He hoped his timing had been right. Where he had felt holes on the flat surface of the indentation, steel bars had begun to rise. In a moment they would cage in the paper, and they were all but snapping into place. But the boom-a-rang did its job well. It arched right through that indentation and swung towards him, catching up the paper with one of its edges just before the steel bars closed off the space, and it spun back to him, bringing the paper with it.

Max caught the boom-a-rang and, just as deftly, grabbed the piece of paper stuck to it. He quickly glanced up as the steel bars collided. If he hadn't used the boom-a-rang, the paper would have been locked inside a steel trap. His hand could have been caught just as easily.

But he had not been caught, and he had extracted the prize.

Max smiled as he read the paper.

You passed again, Mr. Holmes. Please head to the exit and pick up your updated detective certificate. Thank you and have a wonderful day! Oh, by the way . . .

Suddenly water poured down from the ceiling. Max started to laugh, glad he had taken the precaution of putting on the rain gear. He held the paper tightly in his hand as red lights came on, showing him the exit. Water dripping from the hood of his raincoat. He snatched up his backpack and slung it over his shoulder as he headed for the exit, indicated by the red lights. He waited only a few seconds as a door in the wall next to him slid open, showing him into a hallway that led into Scotland Yard. Or would have, that is, if his way had not been blocked by a veritable wall of a man who had planted himself just outside the door, blocking his way. Max looked up, then up some more, until he reached the man's face.

A huge, bushy handlebar mustache dominated that face, and the arches of the mustache seemed to follow the man's frown.

"Mr. Holmes," the man said, leaning over him slightly. "I see you've outwitted our best maze makers yet again. Solved the puzzle with time to spare."

Max tried to smile, but Officer Jaffrey was just that intimidating and formal that a smile always seemed out of place. "Yes, sir."

"No one else has."

"Beg your pardon? Not even Mum and Dad?"

"Oh, they solved it all right. And they're about the only ones who did . . . before you. Ran the course just before they left on assignment, but they exceeded the time limit by nearly three minutes."

He'd hear about that when his folks came back home. Mum was usually okay when Max pulled off amazing feats of deductive gymnastics, but Max knew his father tended to tighten his jaw so that his, "Congratulations, son," always sounded like, "Goll darn cheeky upstart." Then his mum would smother him in kisses, and his dad would allow that the genes were certainly strong in him. It'd been a long time in a long line of Holmes that problem solving and deductive reasoning had come together so strongly in one person. His dad had made a name for himself in Scotland Yard. So had his mum. But only when Mitchem Holmes and Martha Berg finally married and started their family did they realize that their combined capabilities had come together with a particularly awesome impact. Both Max and his sister Mia had been unable to contain in crib, playpen or even a locked room since they had begun to toddle about. They could pick any lock, open any door, figure out any puzzle presented to them. It was just the way their minds worked.

But all that might have gone unnoticed for years yet except for the Doxy Gambit. Right down in the same subbasement where he stood with Officer Jaffrey, Max had solved a series of questions and mazes that was considered the ultimate test of a good deductive agent. He'd been nine at the time, and his mother, who had brought Max to the office with her out of self-defense (his birthday party was in an hour, and she really didn't want him to find his gift beforehand), but he had wandered off and made his way into the maze. When he came out the other end (in record time) no one could believe he had solved the Doxy Gambit, which had confounded dozens of seasoned officers. He had to do it again with half the force in tow just to prove it wasn't a fluke. When he did, even his father had to admit that he lived up to the family name and, maybe, was the match of that famous Holmes of two centuries before.

And so, though Scotland Yard didn't particularly like the idea of a nine-year-old besting them, over the next few years, they began to call on Max when they had a case that stumped even their best officers. These cases had taken Max and his sister all over the world.

Max was very pleased with himself, satisfied with the outcome of the exercise. He had bested a very elaborate system. Again. In so doing, he had proved himself again to the department, reminding disbelieving officers and skeptics that a fourteen-year-old could beat them and that the name Holmes was a force to be reckoned with.

Officer Jaffrey thrust out an ID card, his huge hand nearly engulfing the small laminated rectangle. Max took it from him. On it he saw his name, Maxwell Sherlock Holmes, his ID number, and the line: Certified Officer.

Max looked up into that imposing face. "You had this ready?"

Only then did the handlebars of the mustache widen, stretching over the unseen lips in a wide smile. "I won the bet, too. Netted me nearly fifty pounds, you did. I thank you for that."

Max laughed and joined Officer Jaffrey in the elevator that would whisk him up to the street-level offices. The drill was over and now it was time to go home. Another success!

TWO

AN HOUR LATER MAX WALKED through the front door of his house on Baker Street in London. At fourteen, he still had the features of a young teenager, more boy than adult, and yet every once in a while one could see glimpses of the man he would soon be trying to break through. In other ways, his medium brown hair, trimmed neatly around his ears, and his modest height didn't make him look very imposing, and Max doubted he'd get much taller than his father, who, at five-foot-eight, was no Officer Jaffrey. Still his dark-blue eyes always sparkled with eagerness, and he had an attentive look about him. But, for one so young, Max had already traveled around the world twice, learned a great deal from different places and cultures, and risen in rank at Scotland Yard from the cute "mascot" card he carried when he was just nine to "certified officer," a title he had earned two years before and maintained, even with the department's rigorous tests. He was great—some might say gifted—at observation and deduction. His skill at figuring out puzzles and mysteries was quite remarkable.

"So, how did you do on your detective test?" asked Max's sister, Mia, without looking up as he came into the living room. Mia was two years younger than her brother and was the spitting image of her mother with her blonde hair, pixy face and fair complexion. She would be no basketball star at her height either, but Max feared she might edge taller than he was—as it was, she matched his height inch for inch, though, fortunately, since she insisted on wearing her hair in braids to keep it away from her face, she had more of a child-look than he did. Mia's genius was solving puzzles, especially cryptograms. They were her specialty.

Max took off his cape and hat and hung them up on a peg on the wall next to Mia's and dropped his backpack onto the floor before coming into the living room or answering his sister.

He planted himself before her and planted his fists on his hips in a very Superman kind of pose. With brotherly bravado, he said, "It was easy—as usual. It took me a little time to reason it out at the end, but I finally got it, and with time to spare." It had been thirty-one seconds, but that was really a very comfortable margin. "The inspector said I was the only one who passed the test so far. For my detective renewal they wanted to try something harder this year so they made me solve a fictitious case as well, sat me down with a bunch of disconnected bits of information and a list of suspects. I'll admit it was challenging, but I still solved it within a few hours. That was this morning. After lunch I got to run the maze. They said that most people got so far and then realized that they'd chosen the wrong items to help them. You can't go back once you pass the different levels, so you're pretty much out of luck if you made a mistake." Mimicking the old knight's voice in *Indiana Jones*, he added, "I chose wisely."

"What did you choose?" asked Mia, fixing her large blue eyes on him.

"There were lots of stuff to choose from: a hammer, a butterfly net, a matchbook, a three-wheel cart—maybe a dozen different things."

Mia's expression tilted as she scowled in sisterly fashion. "So . . . what did you choose?"

"A small rubber ball, a boom-a-rang, and a raincoat," replied Max.

"That seems fairly random. Well, I guess the raincoat would explain why you look a little bit damp. So, you chose those things based on clues?"

"Of course, and I guessed them right, too, which is why I chose the items that I did," replied Max. "Which, of course, means my certificate is updated." Max held out the card proudly.

Now Mia gave him a wide smile. "I'm very proud of you," she said and hopped up to gave her brother a big hug. Max returned the hug and glanced past his sister to the other occupant in the room, a woman in her sixties sitting on the sofa against the far wall and knitting what looked like to be a sweater. The colors were a mixture of purple and yellow, but the shapeless mass had one arm longer than the other. Of course it could be a union suit for all he knew and the longer piece really a legging. Not that it mattered. Max couldn't help but smile as he watched the woman's thin features tighten as she concentrated on her task, her bright blue eyes focusing on the needles in her hands, her pink tongue protruding just a bit with the effort. Chances were that she hadn't even noticed he'd come into the room

"Hello, Granny!" said Max.

The woman looked up, blinking like a turtle in sunshine. "Oh, hello, dear. Passed your test, did you? I knew you could do it." Granny gratefully set down her knitting with an added thrust of frustration, rose from the sofa, and went to Max to give him a hug.

She wasn't tall either, but Max still stood almost a full inch shorter than she. Granny was thin, too, looking as though the wind could blow her down with the tiniest puff, but she was actually quite strong, and she moved with a quickness that belied her years. Her mind was also as sharp as a tack. Granny she might be—and she liked to go by that to put people at their ease and also to get into places and under noses unnoticed. "Unassuming is always best," she loved to say. She was very clever—a Holmes through and through. She was a terrific problem solver. As Granny pulled away, Max stared at her.

Granny was considered eccentric. Her disposition was sweet and cheerful, but she had her own unique way of doing things, ways which were usually a bit different from everybody else's in the family. She wore clothes that often didn't match, and she kept her hair in a bun on the top of her head held in place by chopsticks. It always seemed to be crooked. She insisted on knitting things, but rarely could anyone actually wear what she made. She would neglect to put in a neck hole or knit three arms. Knitting was her nemesis, and she did battle with the knitting needles regularly, determined to win out.

Granny patted Max on the cheek, then headed into the kitchen. Max glanced at the desk in the far corner of the room and noticed several layers of newspapers. He then turned to Mia and asked, "What were you working on today?"

Mia glanced over at the desk as well. "Well, I got up, enjoyed the telly—those cooking shows are so much fun—"

"Mia," said Max with warning in his tone. His sister loved to describe her day in the smallest of details.

"I walked out to the post, but there wasn't a new letter from Mum. Did you know the Talberts have a new dog?"

"Mia, I'm warning you."

She rolled her eyes, "Oh, all right," she said and stomped over to the desk, scooping up the paper. "I imagine you were brilliant getting through the tests today. You always are, but it took me only ten minutes to solve today's cryptogram," Mia said as she proudly held out the paper to him. Max was just reaching to take it from her and see the completed cryptogram, when both he and Mia were startled by a loud, almost forceful knock on the door.

THREE

"COME IN," CALLED MAX as he looked to the door. Mia and Max turned as their friend Morris, the computer genius of the group, staggered into the room, his arms so full, Max suspected he had kicked the door. Morris set down two laptop cases, several large books and a grease-soaked, mostly empty sack of popcorn.

"Have you seen today's newspaper?" Morris asked everyone excitedly. He stared at them through his round glasses, a fourteen-year-old that screamed geek, with his messy, longish dark hair, pale complexion, untucked shirt, mismatched socks, and untied shoes. Nearly as tall as Max's father, Morris was as skinny as a bean pole, nervous as a frightened rabbit, and always had a handkerchief sticking halfway out his back pocket, though he seldom could find it when he started sneezing.

"Yes, of course," replied Mia, her nose just a little in the air. "And I solved today's *gold*-level cryptogram. If you ask me, it was too easy. They really need to come up with something a little more challenging."

Morris blinked at her a moment, then rolled his eyes at her indulgently. "Not the *local* paper. Gees, anyone with half a brain can solve those cryptograms. I mean the *world* paper—the one on the Internet. Solve the cryptograms in there, and I'll really be impressed." When neither Max nor Mia seemed to know what he was talking about, Morris's shoulders slumped. "Don't you two ever look at your computers?"

Morris pulled a bunch of papers out of his other back pocket, and he tossed these towards Max, who caught them easily. Granny returned to the living room with a glass of ice water. She was heading back to her knitting.

"Good afternoon, Granny," said Morris.

"Oh, Morris. How are you, dear?" Granny replied as she took a sip from her glass and sat on the sofa.

"I'm just fine. Your grandchildren, however, could stand a bit of education. Tell me that *you* at least checked out the *World News Quarterly* on-line," said Morris.

"Oh, please," said Granny with a laugh. "I'm what you'd call computer illiterate. Don't even know how to turn the thing on. If you want to install something useful on that thing, put the Clapper on it. Then maybe I'd use it now and again. Back in my day, computers were called books, and those I can find my way around just fine, thanks. Anyway, I leave the computer stuff up to Max, Mia, and . . . and you . . . to tell me what's going on in the world," said Granny, and she twiddled her fingers at her grandchildren.

"And Mia and I leave all the *heavy* computer stuff to you, Morris," said Max with a grin. "Frankly, I have more important things to do with my time than to stare at a computer screen all day," he said. "No offense, Morris, old buddy. I know you think they're God's gift in that arena, but I just like to get out and about. Not a sit-still kind of guy, I guess."

"That goes for me, too. Staring at a computer screen for hours hurts my eyes," added Mia. "Sorry but, though the Internet is filled with information, I'd just rather solve puzzles and read books."

Morris shook his head and ran his fingers through his long brown hair and then gazed back at his friends with exasperation. "If it's a question of the screen hurt-ing your eyes, I can set up a special screen so the light won't tire your eyes, and then I can modify the—" The trio of blank stares halted him. "Fine, fine. I get it. You'd think I'd learn not to try to educate you guys, but it's your loss. And, yes, as long as my effort is appreciated, I'll still keep you informed, even against my better judgement."

"Thanks, Morris," Mia said sweetly.

Max had spread the papers Morris had tossed him on the desk, trying to smooth them enough to read them. Mia looked at them, a little puzzled by what she saw. On the front page was a large picture of a decorative sock, and right on top of it was a question mark. Before Mia could read the article, Max seemed to change his mind and took the papers to the couch. Mia and Max sat next to Granny and opened the papers so she could see them, too. She glanced at them, got interested and set down her knitting to take up the papers and peruse them quickly. She then handed them to Mia, who read the article aloud, holding the papers so everyone could see.

"Mr. Charles Delacomb, the owner of Delacomb Cereal Company and the maker of the popular Rainbow O's and Rocky Wheat Crunch cereal, had a robbery at his country estate in Naples, Florida, last night. Stolen was an antique green sock, said to have been Elvis Presley's grandmother's. The sock had been bought at auction a year ago for rumored six-digit price. More on page five." Mia quickly turned to the next page and found the continuation of the article. But instead of reading the article aloud, she read it to herself, as did Max and Granny.

"How peculiar," said Max. "It seems that the police haven't a clue who pulled off this job, or why. The sock was kept in Mr. Delacomb's library, though they're not saying exactly where in his library, but in the sock's place lying next to the matching one, was a cryptogram." Max thought for a moment before saying, "If the pair of socks was so valuable, why would the robber leave the one?"

"Why would anyone take an old sock in the first place?" asked Mia, ignoring Max. Everyone ignored Max. He usually talked aloud, focusing his words on no one in particular. "Someone took one of a pair of socks and left a cryptogram. Someone's fooling the police with cryptograms."

"I'm assuming the cryptogram couldn't be solved," said Granny, looking up at Morris.

"No, but that's not the interesting part. My research indicates that the police checked out the estate for intruders, checking for fingerprints and so on, but they found no evidence that led to any suspect. They even had the paper the cryptogram was written on analyzed, but that turned up nothing. Before any more work could be completed, Mr. Delacomb asked for the cryptogram back and dismissed the police, effectively closing the investigation, but . . ." Morris gave this a dramatic pause and waited until he had everyone's attention. "Now he's coming *here* for answers."

Mia and Max gazed at each other before turning their attention back to Morris, saying in unison, "Here? When?"

"Today—sometime this afternoon I imagine. He's flying in on his personal jet. My resources say that Mr. Delacomb is looking to solve this case quickly and with as little publicity as possible. He doesn't want the world to know of his problems and wishes to keep the information about the sock a secret. He's checked up on us and knows of our abilities. He wants to hire us to solve his case."

Though all three opened their mouths to speak, someone knocked on the door. After glancing at each other, Granny stood and went to answer the door. When she opened it, a tall, portly gentleman, in an expensive gray suit with matching cravat, stepped inside. Black-haired and with small glasses hung low on his long nose, his appearance spoke of importance.

"Can I help you, sir?" asked Granny.

"Yes! I'm looking for the detectives who call themselves the Crypto-Capers. I was told they lived here. Are they in?" asked the man.

"I'm Nellie Holmes, and these are my grandchildren, Max and Mia," replied Granny as Max and Mia came forward. "This is Morris Weedlesom. Together we  are the Crypto-Capers. Please come in." Showing some relief, the man stepped inside. Granny ushered him into the living room, offered him a seat, which he took, and refreshment, which he declined.

"An unusual name—the Crypto-Capers."

"It's kind of a listing of our skills and what we do," offered Morris. "Crypto is short for cryptograms, ah, messages written in a code or cipher. Caper can mean a playful trick. We were thinking along the lines of playing with cryptograms and solving cases, hence the name, the Crypto-Capers."

The man nodded as he glanced around the room nervously. "You were recommended to me by a friend— Lord Barege?"

Max gave a laugh. "Yes, we know Lord Barege. He's a friend of my parents." They had solved a case for him a few years ago.

Still nervous, the man said, "I didn't know I'd be dealing with . . . children. Perhaps it's your parents . . . forgive me. I really don't mean to be rude, but . . . aren't your parents known for their talents at solving cases that . . . shall we say, are impossible?"

Max burned just a bit inside. He could solve the most elaborate tests, and yet he wasn't taken seriously because he was fourteen. Still, he responded politely. "They're away on another case at present. We don't expect them back for another week or so."

"So I was told. I'm disappointed not to find them here, of course, because I'm in need of their services. But Lord Barege sent me here anyway. He told me that you and the rest of the . . . Crypto-Capers would be able to help me." The man paused and ran his tongue over his lips as if they had dried. "Do you . . . do you know who I am?"

Such an obvious question. The man might as well have a nametag pinned on his breast pocket. Max almost rolled his eyes. Instead he replied, "You're Mr. Delacomb, sir, the owner of Delacomb Cereal Company. We like your Rainbow O's, by the way."

Mr. Delacomb glanced towards Max and smiled, pleased that his identity was known. It seemed to relieve some of his nerves. "Splendid!" he said. "Then you know why I'm here?"

"Not exactly. We know you had an antique sock stolen from your estate in Florida. What we don't know is why the sock was so important."

Embarrassment forced Mr. Delacomb's glance toward the ground. "The importance is not held so much with the sock, as what was hidden inside it. Don't get me wrong, the sock is very valuable. It was once owned by Elvis Presley's grandmother." Mr. Delacomb raised his head and whispered. "I bought it at an auction a year ago for a really good price." He then cleared his throat, his features turning more serious. "Inside the sock was a one-of-a-kind pair of black, diamond-studded, Prada sunglasses. The top edge was solid gold while the rest was black onyx. I had them made special for my wife for her birthday. I had hidden them—she's such an old snoop. Needless to say, the glasses cost me a small fortune."

"Mr. Delacomb," started Mia. "This may be a silly question, but why did you put the sunglasses in the sock?"

Mr. Delacombs forehead wrinkled slightly as if he were not sure on how to answer the question.

"She'd never look for them there," he said with a shrug. "You might find this strange but I told my wife that she couldn't buy any more sunglasses. She's obsessed with them, has hundreds of them. And not the twenty-dollar kind either. Not even the hundred-dollar ones. No, my wife spends thousands of dollars on sunglasses, and she doesn't even wear them. Somehow that would 'spoil' them. She adds them to her collection. Personally, I don't get it." Mr. Delacomb shook his head in obvious frustration. "Her hobby has become so costly, I felt I needed to put a stop to it. I told her she had to stop or seek some kind of glasses-anonymous organization. She was furious with me, of course, that I'd think her 'hobby' was a disease and swore she'd prove to me that she could stop. And, I must say, she's not purchased a single pair of glasses since.

"However, her birthday's coming up, and I thought that buying her a singular pair of sunglasses would let her know how proud I am of her. I mean, the one pair she actually will wear is . . . well, you see, I broke them. I accidentally sat on them in the car. What the sunglasses were doing on the seat, I don't know. She usually hangs them from her visor, but . . ." Mr. Delacomb took a deep breath.

"Now, knowing her birthday is in a few days, she's been searching the house from top to bottom for my present to her. She's sneaky, too. And she usually finds the gifts I hide, which is why I hid the sunglasses in the antique sock. She rarely goes into the library, which is where I keep the socks. They hang inside one of my curio cabinets. And, frankly, she thinks it odd and disgusting that I would display such a thing. I honestly didn't think she would find them there. I don't think she actually took them, but someone did and—"

"When's your wife's birthday?" asked Mia.

"September eighth."

"Did you ask your wife about the sunglasses when they went missing?" asked Granny.

"Yes! Yes, of course. She was the first person I asked, but she had no idea what I was talking about, thought I believed she had taken my old sock. Then I had to explain what was *in* the sock, and she became quite excited, yet disappointed, of course, that such a wonderful pair sunglasses had been stolen. She wanted them desperately, thought they would be the culminating addition to her collection." Mia, Max, and Morris glanced at each other while Mr. Delacomb reached into his pocket. He showed them a piece of paper. "I found this in the missing sock's place in my curio cabinet." He offered the slip of paper to Granny. With Mia, Max, and Morris looking on, Granny glanced at it.

September 5th

"The thief left you a cryptogram," said Max, "and it's dated two days from now."

"Yes, and because my wife's birthday's just three days after that, you can see the bind I'm in. I don't know what to do. I don't know how to solve this sort of thing . . . or even what it's supposed to mean," said Mr.

Delacomb, sounding helpless. "I'd like to hire the Crypto-Capers to retrieve my wife's sunglasses and to find the thief responsible for taking them and causing me so much trouble. I mean, the police have been all over this, but they think it's a joke. They're looking for an old lady's sock, for heaven's sake. Telling them about the glasses, well . . . I don't need a scandal or . . . to be made out as an old fool, so your discretion's important."

"Just how valuable are these glasses?" Max asked.

The man hemmed and hawwed. "Well, they're a singular piece of art, and then there's the gold and jewels and—"

"Please, Mr. Delacomb. We must know what we're dealing with."

He sighed. "Well, there's the Hope diamond and then . . ." He left the rest to their imaginations. "If the news ever got out about these sunglasses, if someone found out about the cryptogram, people would be crawling over everything to get them. I may never get them back then. At this moment, you might be the only ones who can help me."

Granny glanced at Mia, Max, and Morris, who were still quite stunned at the value of a pair of glasses, and smiled. They loved an adventure, and solving crimes were their favorite pastime.

"We accept the case, Mr. Delacomb, but we need to start at the beginning. We'll need to go to your estate in Florida to look for clues. Mia can solve the cryptogram if we need her too, but we're going to wait to see if there's a key.

Ciphers are used to code and decode messages. The number in the code could be changed to mean something else. Most cryptograms have a key to decode the message. I'd bet that somewhere in your home is the key to this cryptogram. And where there's one cryptogram, there are surely others. We'll need the key then more than ever," said Granny.

The gentleman pointed to the door. "I have a private jet waiting for us, so . . . whenever you're ready," said Mr. Delacomb anxiously, as if they should walk out that very moment.

Granny handed the cryptogram to Max, who slipped it into his pocket. They quickly ran to pack for the trip. Granny called after them, reminding them not to forget their passports.

Max packed quickly with only his basic clothing needs, something he had learned from his travels. Then, he grabbed their equipment bag and packed it with all of the essentials, as well as with some miscellaneous items he thought they'd need. He spent considerably more time doing this than shoving his clothes into a black grip. With the equipment bag in one hand and his much smaller grip in the other, he was ready and headed for the door, where Mr. Delacomb, Mia, and Morris were already waiting. As Max and Mia donned their hats and capes, Granny came out of her room.

They had to wait a few more minutes while Granny hastily straightened up the house, returning her water glass to the kitchen and putting away the breakfast things.

"Don't worry about the mess, Granny," Morris said. "I'll put things away."

Granny quickly turned to face him. "You don't want to come with us *again*?" Granny asked.

"It's the flying, Granny. Anyway, I can run things from here," answered Morris.

"Yes, but——" started Granny.

"Granny, I'd much prefer to do this my way. When have I ever traveled comfortably with you guys? We go somewhere by car and pretty soon I'm standing on the top of some dizzy height, and I'm afraid of heights. We go out to some big, flat field, and my asthma kicks up. We're at the seaside, and I step on a jellyfish. We go to the middle of London, and a bee stings me, and I have to be rushed to hospital because I'm allergic—plain and simple, I just don't do well in the field. But it's okay, I really rather enjoy staying behind. All of my equipment's here, along with my research. I'm more useful if I stay behind. But, to make you feel better, I've added tracking devices to everyone's luggage, so I can make sure that all of you arrive safely."

Max and Mia rolled their eyes, but Granny kissed Morris on the head. "Oh Morris, you are so handy." She gave Morris a hug and then picked up her plaid bag. She then glanced at her appearance in the mirror, and straightened her hat. While Granny's attention was focused elsewhere Max gave Morris some last minute reminders.

"Keep your watch phone and computer on at all times. I'll be sending you information as we get it."

"I know how to do my part of the job. Just as an FYI though," he said holding out a small, padded case, "I suggest you take your new laptop, and," he added as he handed it over, "please be careful with it. Father says if you break one more that he'll start charging us for repairs and updates. He said to specifically tell you that, under no uncertain terms is a laptop to be used to prop open an elevator or be thrown after an escaping villain. He said to tell you that shoes and rocks work better for that sort of thing."

Max grinned. "I'll do my best to limit how I use it. I know my track record is terrible."

"Scary, actually."

"Yes, we do need to take better care of our equipment," said Granny soothingly. "Not only is it expensive, but it helps us solve our cases." With that said Granny threw her cape around her shoulders. "Shall we be off then?"

Mr. Delacomb led the way as the trio followed him out. Morris waved good-bye, watching his friends walk out to the limo at the curb and hand Mr. Delacomb's driver their luggage. Morris closed the door and moved to the window. He waited until he saw the limo pull away from the curb before turning from the window. Morris then walked over to his laptop, which he had brought with him and was never far from him, and turned it on. After several seconds, Morris began typing furiously. Soon, a map appeared on the screen, as well as three red dots. One dot was Mia. One was Max, and one was Granny. Morris smiled as the tracking devices blinked at him. A cluster of green dots seemed to be following them.

Not only had Morris plant tracking devices on everyone's luggage—the green dots—but he also planted them on their persons as well—the red dots. At their last physicals, required because they traveled frequently, they were all given injections. Morris had given the company doctor the small tracking devices, the width of a small pencil lead point and less than a millimeter in length, and he had planted them in everyone's right shoulder, including his own. Feeling good about his team's safety, Morris decided to make some popcorn and relax as they traveled to the airport and made their flight.

As he began to look for the popcorn in the bottom food cupboard, where it was usually kept, a voice came from his watch phone.

"The popcorn's now in the top cupboard behind the jelly your mother made for us," came Max's voice. Morris grinned and opened the top cupboard, spying the popcorn exactly where Max had said it would be. He grabbed it, closed the cupboard, and said, "Thanks!" When he suddenly realized that Max really had no idea where he was or what he was doing, he stared at his arm.

Max's voice came again from the watch phone. "You're welcome!"

Then Granny said, "Now, Morris, this time make sure that you clean up after yourself. When we returned from our last case, we could practically follow your popcorn trail all the way across town, through the park, down five aisles at the grocery store, and then finally to your house. And you left our house a bloody mess."

Morris's eyes grew wide as he shook his head, then began to laugh. "Okay, okay. Don't worry, by the time you get back I'll have this house spotless. I just want all of you to promise to be careful."

"Don't worry, dear, we will," replied Granny.

Though Morris's concern was for everyone, he was specifically concerned for Granny. She had a bad habit of wondering around where she was not suppose to, and at times had gotten lost. That was another reason why she wore a tracking device. Morris then turned his attention back to his popcorn, but he couldn't find the popcorn popper. As he stood in the kitchen, dumfounded, Mia's voice came through the watch phone. "It's underneath the sink. The butter's in the fridge. The salt's above the sink but use the sea salt, it tastes better, and the big blue bowl you love is in the dishwasher."

"Thanks, everyone," said Morris.

"You're welcome," replied Granny, Mia, and Max in unison. Morris started to laugh. His friends knew him so well.

FOUR

AFTER A LONG DAY of travel, Max, Mia, and Granny made it to Florida and had a nice rest in a comfortable hotel before a limo arrived to take them to Mr. Delacomb's estate. As the limo began to slow in front of a large estate with an ornate wrought-iron gate. The driver pulled into the driveway and stopped before the twelve-foot barrier. He inserted a key card into a box. After several seconds the gate opened, and the limo cruised up the driveway and pulled up in front of the main entrance to a house that looked like a southern plantation. As everyone climbed out, Max glanced at Mr. Delacomb and asked, "Who else has a key to the gate?"

"My wife and son have keys, of course, as well as my driver, the cook, the cleaning woman, and the landscaper. The keys cannot be duplicated, and each time a key is used it's logged into my security system."

"Seven keys. That's a lot, really," Max said.

"Besides your rather impressive fence, do you have a security system in your house as well?" asked Granny.

Mr. Delacomb looked a little uncomfortable. "Well, no, the gate is my only security system. Thus far it's worked out perfectly. This is the first theft I've had."

"Was it working the day of the theft?" Mia asked.

Mr. Delacomb nodded vigorously. "The police already checked the system and verified that everyone who used a gate key that day was checked out and questioned."

Max had made note of two cameras at the gate, one on each major support pillar. "Can we look at the security tape?" asked Max.

"Unfortunately, no. It was erased by accident. When the police looked at the tape, the system reset itself. It's a glitch in the system we didn't know we had, and have rectified."

A servant opened the front door as they crossed a wide veranda. Granny, last in line to enter the house, noticed a large crystal chandelier in the vaulted foyer and the polished marble floors. Every piece of furniture looked like it was out of a Chippendale magazine.

"This way please," said Mr. Delacomb. "I'll warn you that the police have already been here searching for clues—dusting their powder everywhere. They didn't find anything though. I'm hoping you'll be able to tell me something . . . anything."

Max and Mia followed Mr. Delacomb, but Granny didn't. Instead, she slipped back outside before the servant closed the door.

Mr. Delacomb led the way up the circular staircase to the library on the second floor. The room was closed off. The door still had yellow tape across it. Mr. Delacomb removed the tape and opened the door. Max and Mia followed him inside. Max stepped into the room, placing their equipment bag onto the floor near the door. Mia, distracted by the detailed molding around the door, tripped on the edge of the equipment bag. She instantly reached out and grabbed onto the door frame to steady herself. She noticed that her fingertips were just a bit sticky. She immediately brought her fingertips to her nose and noticed the sweet scent of maple syrup.

Mia glanced at the wall before moving hastily to their equipment bag. She rummaged through the bag removing a brush and some black powder from a small plastic tote. She then hurried back to the door frame and dusted it for prints. There was none, only a smudge of a partial wrist could be seen. Mia frowned. Her slip might just have destroyed evidence, and she hated that. She hastily pulled out a pad of paper from her pocket and made a note before returning the powder and brush to the bag. She then turned quickly around to warn Granny about the molding but realized that she wasn't there.

"Granny?" Mia called as she stood in the hallway looking around. Mia then poked her head into the library, thinking that Granny might have entered without her noticing, but she wasn't in the library either. "Max, do you know where Granny went?"

Max quickly glanced around the room to the other. "No, but you know Granny. She probably wandered off somewhere looking for clues."

Mia shrugged and nodded, and began to look around the library.

Max had made a few notes and turned his attention back to Mr. Delacomb. "Now, Mr. Delacomb, can you please tell us exactly what happened, and don't leave anything out. It may be very important," said Max.

"Well, when I first came home with the sunglasses, the gift for my wife, I hurried up here to hide them. This library's my favorite place in the house, and I spend a lot of time here. It's *my* place, if you will. I keep some business files in this room, as well as a few valuables—the safe's in here."

"And why didn't you put the glasses in the safe?" Max asked.

Mr. Delacomb shrugged. "My wife has the combination, too, and we were going to dinner that night. She keeps her best jewelry in there." He paused, a little embarrassed, then pointed across the room. "If you look over there in the curio cabinet you'll see the remaining sock."

Indeed, when Max and Mia walked closer to the curio cabinet, they saw a large decorative green sock, the same one they had seen in the paper.

"I know you must still be wondering why I'd hide the sunglasses in the sock, especially when there're literally dozens of other places that I could have hid them and the safe where they'd be secure, but to me it made perfect sense. My wife rarely comes in here except to go to the safe, and because she doesn't have the key to the cabinet, I figured that it would be safe there. Especially when she thinks my socks are gross and ridiculous. Apparently, someone thought to look there for them."

"Did anyone see you put the sunglasses in the sock?" asked Mia.

"I don't believe so. I closed the door before I hid them, at least I thought I did, but I could be mistaken. It might not have been *completely* shut. And no one knew I'd purchased them—except the broker I ordered them from . . . and maybe his secretary . . . oh, and my chauffeur, of course . . . and the housekeeper because she was cleaning in the hall when I got here."

Max sighed.

"But, as soon as I saw the sock, I just knew it was the right place to hide the glasses, and no one saw that. At least I don't think anyone did. But, you know, now that I really think about it, I might not have closed the door at all, but the housekeeper had gone down stairs, and no one else was around, at least I don't think anyone was." Mr. Delacomb thought about it for a moment longer, but his face didn't clear. Then he brightened and said, "But, but I'm almost certain I locked the door when I left the room."

Max glanced around the room and noticed a large window. It was currently closed. "Could the thief have entered in through the window?" Max asked.

"Oh, I think that highly unlikely. As the house is built on a slope and we're on the second floor, it's three floors to the ground."

"And you have no ladders that can reach the window?" Max asked.

"Well, sure, but—"

"But, what, Mr. Delacomb?"

"Surely no one suspects members of my family or staff."

"Everyone's a suspect until eliminated," Max offered.

Mr. Delacomb paled, clearly unhappy with that idea. After a pause, he said, "As you can clearly see from all the powder, the police have already dusted for fingerprints, they found nothing."

Mia said, "How long after you had hidden the glasses did they disappear?"

"Well, I can't know that exactly. I put them into the sock about ten that morning, and I noticed they were gone . . . it was that evening . . . about 10:30 when we came back from dinner and I came up here to fax a few forms to my office. The odd thing is that a thief could have just slipped out the glasses, and I might not have noticed until I was ready to wrap them. But the thief took the sock as well. And just the one sock. I don't get that. I saw right away when I entered the room and sat down at my desk. I looked over and saw that one sock was missing. When I opened the cabinet, I realized the sunglasses were gone too."

"And the window was closed?" Mia asked.

"Oh, yes. It gets so hot on the west side of the house. The air conditioning would never keep up if I left windows open."

"But was it locked?" Max asked.

For a moment, Mr. Delacomb stared at him. Then he shook his head with uncertainty. "The police have already spoken to my entire family as well as the servants, and they all have alibis. How the thief entered was where they were stuck, too, I'm afraid," said Mr. Delacomb.

Before another question could be asked, a tapping sound drew everyone's attention to the window in question. The tapping was quiet at first, almost polite, then slowly worked up to a glass-rattling pounding.

Max walked over to the window and drew aside the curtains. Mia screamed. All eyes stared at the window in surprise. Granny's face looked in on them. She pushed up her glasses and said, "Would you be a dear, Maxy, and open the window?"

"Granny?" Max shouted. Granny was standing on a ladder waving at them. Max opened the window. "What are you doing out there, Granny?" He looked down. "That's a very tall ladder."

Granny's smile faltered, and she struggled to get into the library. Max and Mia each grabbed an arm and helped her inside. Granny straightened her dress, pushed her glasses up again and smiled as if she loved the excitement, ignoring that she could have fallen three stories.

"What lovely grounds you have, Mr. Delacomb. I was curious about the outside of the mansion and looked for clues on the outside of the house. You two would have everything covered in here, of course. Besides, I found what I was looking for." Granny extended her arm toward the window.

"The ladder?" asked Mia.

"Well, yes and no. The reason why I used this ladder was because I found ladder imprints below this window. I took a picture of them, of course, so we can confirm them with Morris. The ladder was lying on the ground near some window washing equipment. I dusted it for prints but it was clean. The imprints on the ground were slight indentations only, though, which made me wonder about them," said Granny. "So I placed the ladder underneath the window, away from the evidence of course, and thought to climb it to prove my point."

"What was the point?" asked Mr. Delacomb.

"Oh, to prove that the ladder was lightly stepped on and not climbed. When I climbed the ladder it made much deeper indentations then the ones I found, which tells me that someone was *going* to use the ladder and then decided against it. Could it have been the thief? Possibly! Or it could have been the window washers? But if it was the washers, I'd have found more prints on the ladder. They usually don't wear gloves when washing windows. They also usually use platforms, not ladders, which makes me think that this ladder is not theirs or, at least, not used for that purpose." Mr. Delacomb hurried to the window and glanced down at the ladder.

"The washers were going to start the next morning, but, what with the investigation, that order was cancelled. The ladder's mine. The gardener uses it to trim the trees. It's usually kept in the shed. There's no reason for it to be out here. There haven't been any storm or . . . anyway, the washers bring their own equipment"

All eyes focused on Mr. Delacomb. Granny started to chuckle softly, and focus shifted to her. "Then, perhaps we should take a look at that shed," she said with certainty. "There may be something in there that'll help us. What did you find in here?"

"Not too much," Max said. "Mia might have found something by the doorway, but that's about it. Before we saw you, Mr. Delacomb was telling us how the window had nothing to do with the crime, but now the evidence is telling us otherwise." Max paced across the room, turning back. "Or," he said, "it could be leading us astray. The one thing I'm learning about this case is that nothing is what it appears." Max shook his head and placed his hands on his hips. "You said you took pictures of the indentations you made with the ladder?"

Granny removed her camera from her handbag.

"Good!" Max then raised his left arm. "Morris!" he bellowed into his watch phone.

"You do realize that you don't have to shout," came Morris's petulant reply. "That's a sensitive microphone in that watch. It could pick up the sound of a pin dropping over by the curio case, which you are not presently near. You're standing in front of the open window. I can hear the wind through the trees outside . . . live oaks, I presume. Oops! I just dropped my eggs," said Morris through the watch phone.

"Sorry!" said Max. "They're walnut trees, though, I believe." Max was about to say more when he thought about something. "Did you say that you just dropped eggs?"

"Yes! For some reason I was craving them for supper, it must mean that my body needs the protein to support my large muscles." There was a pause. Max knew it was because Morris was probably flexing his muscles like a wrestler. Max started to laugh. Then Morris added, "I'm going to assume that you rescued Granny from the ladder. I told her not to climb it."

Max glanced at Granny, who shrugged and shook her head as if she knew nothing of what they were talking about.

"Yes, we found her. She's fine. She may have ruled out the window as access."

"The photos clearly tell that story. By the way, Mr. Delacomb's mansion's huge."

Mr. Delacomb, his mouth hanging open, said, "Morris? The boy we left in England? How could he possibly know where Nellie was or . . . or anything about my home?"

"He uses a satellite connection, Mr. Delacomb. Granny gets lost a lot," explained Max.

"I do not," said Granny in a huff. "I've never been lost once in my life. I go exploring for clues and evidence. That's not lost. It's just that . . . sometimes my exploring . . . well, it takes me into places where I shouldn't be sometimes."

"Like the time you found yourself in that maze that took you several hours to negotiate," offered Mia.

"To this day I'm still not sure how I got in there." Granny shook her head.

"Or the time you tripped the entrance of a secret room and was locked in there until we solved the case," Max said.

Granny pointed a bony finger at him. "Being locked up isn't being lost, and you know it."

"Or the time—" Mia began.

"She gets lost!" Mr. Delacomb blurted.

Granny pursed her lips and folded her arms over her chest.

"But this time, Granny did find evidence," Mia said soothingly.

"Morris, did you hear that?" asked Max into his watch phone.

"Yes! Ladder imprints," said Morris. "Got them. But what did you find, Mia?"

"Something sticky on the door jam. It was just on the outside of the molding. I doubt the police noticed it. Can you analyze that? Or maybe just confirm that it's maple syrup?"

"I can do that for you," called Morris. "Mia, I placed a compact gas spectrometer in your equipment bag. It is in the black case. Press the substance to the input port and send it across the Internet to me."

Mia walked over to their equipment bag and pulled out the black case. She opened it on Mr. Delacombs desk. In just a few moments, she had pressed her still sticky fingertips to the port and sent the analysis of the substance to Morris.

"Got it," said Morris's disembodied voice. "Yes, maple syrup . . . the real stuff, too. Imported from Vermont."

Mr. Delacomb's mouth was hanging again. "It's the only kind we use—"

"You're incredible, Morris. Have I told you that lately?" said Mia.

"At least a dozen times, but I still like hearing it," remarked Morris, his voice preening.

"Don't you need us to send the pictures Granny took?" Max asked.

They could hear Morris yawn. "The cameras have Internet connection already. I get them as soon as you take them. Duh."

"I knew you were a part of the team for a reason, Morris. You're bloody brilliant," said Max into his watch.

"Yes, well, someone has to pick up the technological slack around here. If it were up to you three, you'd still be using a magnifying glass and collecting evidence in little Baggies. I mean, geez."

The trio rolled their eyes.

Then Max walked over to the curio cabinet.

"Mr. Delacomb," Max said in a firm voice, "can you open this door please?"

FIVE

MR. DELACOMB WALKED OVER to his desk, opened a drawer, slid aside a small panel in the side of the oak and pulled out a key. He then gave Max a curious look and walked over to the cabinet and unlocked it.

"Do you usually keep your key in there?" asked Mia, pointing towards the drawer.

"Yes, I have that secret compartment hidden in the side of the drawer. No one knows it's there but me."

Mia put on a pair of gloves and studied the drawer, checking for fingerprints. When she found none, she began to write on her notepad. In the meantime, Max opened the door of the curio cabinet and glanced at the assortment of odd things Mr. Delacomb thought interesting enough to display there. The second sock hung there, of course, and he had an old skeleton key, a wood carving of a beluga whale, a beer much with the image of a troll in the bottom of it, an ancient, very worn teddy bear, presumably his own from his childhood, a skate key and a pair of strap on roller skates, and a box decorated with pretty multi-colored flowers, almost like a rose malling. The wooden box's lid was tilted, mostly closed but not quite. It seemed to have caught on something and held partially opened. From the thin layer of dust, Max guessed it had also been moved slightly from its original location.

"Have you touched this lately, sir?" asked Max.

Mr. Delacomb walked closer to the cabinet and bent down low, glancing at the box.

"That's my grandmother's box. She kept odd things in it. Really, you have no idea the stuff she kept."

Max met his sister's eyes across the room. Considering the oddments Mr. Delacomb had, he couldn't begin to guess what his grandmother stored in the box.

"I haven't taken it out in . . . ages. I just keep it for sentimental value I doubt it's worth more than a garage sale trinket."

"You'd be surprised what some garage sale trinkets go for nowadays," Max intoned.

"What's inside now?" asked Granny.

Mr. Delacombs cheeks rose to a flush, and he turned slightly away.

"I hesitate to say. My wife use to write me the sweetest love letters when we were just teens. I keep them in this box to remind me of what an incredible woman she is, and how lucky I am to have her."

"That's really sweet, Mr. Delacomb," said Granny, a hand to her chest. "You're a true romantic."

"Yes, well . . ." began Mr. Delacomb, smiling.

"May we take a glance inside?" asked Max.

"The box? That doesn't have anything to do with the missing glasses or the sock," said Mr. Delacomb, clearly confused.

"Actually, I'm pretty sure it does," replied Max. "If you look closely, you'll see that it's been moved slightly to the left. You can just see the clean line there. I suspect this cabinet doesn't get dusted very often."

"Well, no. I mean, it has a glass front so not too much dust gets in, and then I keep it locked, so the housekeeper has to come to me to get the key to dust it."

Max nodded. "And a good thing that is, too."

"But why would anyone touch that ancient old box?" Mr. Delacomb said, almost pleading for a reason.

Max snapped on a pair of plastic gloves and reached into the cabinet. He very carefully lifted the box and removed it from the cabinet. He set it carefully on Mr. Delacomb's desk and examined it. Only after looking it over minutely and taking pictures of it from all sides for Morris, did Max slowly take off the lid, setting it carefully aside upside down. The sweet scent of peaches and vanilla immediately wafted up from the contents. Max leaned forward and glanced at the colored envelopes nestled inside the box. Most were neatly placed tied with a pink ribbon. Then Max noticed one envelope out of place, one not quite square with the rest. He snapped a shot of that for Morris as well.

"You're very careful with these . . . keep them very neat," Max said.

"Well, they're very special—"

"So why is this one a little cockeyed?"

Mr. Delacomb looked into the box. "No, no, that's wrong. All the envelopes should be pink or green. That one's white."

Max nodded. He reached into the box, and carefully lifted out the ribbon-bound packet of envelopes. He slid the ribbon to the side and thumbed down to the white envelope. Very slowly, he slid it from the stack. Setting the stack down, he turned the envelope over several times. There were no markings, no address. Max then lifted the flap and looked inside. The paper was folded awkwardly with several creases. Max slid it out smoothly and opened it slowly. When he had the sheet of paper fully open, a smile rose to his lips. "Mia?" he said as he turned towards his sister.

Mia, who had been studying the drawer, was at that moment looking at a silver-framed photo of Mr. Delacomb's family that rested on top of the desk. The picture was of Mr. Delacomb, his wife, and their son. When Max called her name, Mia looked up. Max then held up the paper, and Granny and Mia looked over his shoulder. Written on the paper were several letters. Max presented it to Mr. Delacomb. "I believe, sir, that this is the key to your cryptogram," said Max triumphantly as they studied the letters.

A	B	C	D	E	F	G	H	I	J	K	L	M	N	O	P	Q	R	S	T	U	V	W	X	Y	Z
F	E	B	Y	C	M	N	V	O	L	X	A	K	U	P	Q	I	S	G	D	T	J	Z	R	H	W

"What do the letters mean?" asked Mr. Delacomb. "What does it say?"

"Like this? These letters mean nothing as they are. But applied to the cryptogram you found . . ." replied Mia as she held out her hand to her brother, "this key might mean everything."

Max took the hint and not only placed the key into Mia's hand, but the cryptogram that Mr. Delacomb had given to them when they had first met. Mia eagerly spread out both papers side by side on the desk. She pulled a pen from her pocket and began to solve the cryptogram. It took her only a few minutes, even with checking several times to make sure that she didn't make an error, and then she lifted the paper up, saying, "All done!" Max, Granny and Mr. Delacomb hurried to the desk and stared at the cryptogram.

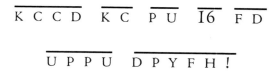

$$\text{K C C D} \quad \text{K C} \quad \text{P U} \quad \overline{\text{16}} \quad \text{F D}$$

$$\text{U P P U} \quad \text{D P Y F H !}$$

" _____ "

(FILL IN YOUR CRYPTOGRAM ANSWER)

48

Mr. Delacomb said, "I don't understand. Today is the fifth of September, yes, but the cryptogram gives no indication of where!"

"Oh, but it does, Mr. Delacomb," replied Max. "It's just that the answer isn't as obvious to us as it should be. We need to look harder to find more clues to figure it out, which is probably what the thief has in mind, but the cryptogram is telling us all we need to know to move ahead."

Max quickly went back to the desk and glanced again at the box, scraping at the edge of the up-turned lid. Then he crossed back over to the cabinet, opened it and looked around. He took out his magnifying lens and studied something on the glass shelf near where the box had been sitting.

The disembodied voice of Morris filled the silence of the room. "Well, you could share the cryptogram with me, you know," Morris said petulantly. "And whatever you just found, Max, I want in on it."

Max laughed. He retrieved tweezers from the equipment bag and picked up a small, thin, shriveled scrap of something. Mia already knew what he was going to do, so she set down the cryptogram and reached for the laptop, rotating the screen to lay flat. Max lay the shriveled bit on the laptop screen.

"What is that?" asked Mr. Delacomb as he pointed towards the screen. "What did you find?"

"I'm not sure. It could be a bit of grass clipping or some kind of herb. It is hard to tell because of its condition. What I do know is that this evidence is not more than two to three days old. It puts it in the timeline of the theft. We'll need Morris's help for this one to be sure. Miraculously enough, he has a database full of various grasses, weeds, herbs, and plants." Max then whispered, "Honestly, sometimes I think he gets bored."

Max then raised his voice louder, "Morris, can you see what I found? Can you identify it?"

For a long moment, everyone waited, but nothing seemed to be happening. "Morris?" Mia called into her watch phone.

Morris's voice instantly boomed back, "I'd prefer it if you didn't yell."

"Did you get our scan?" Max asked, purposely keeping his voice conversational.

"Of course, I got it. Give me a minute to identify it. Oh, now that's interesting."

"What? What?" Max and Mia asked in unison.

"Well, first things first. I have the results from the pictures Granny took. The first marks on the grass are from an extension ladder. The only way those indentations could have been made was if someone stood on it briefly, maybe not applying all their weight, as if they were interrupted or suddenly realized that the marks could give them away. The second indentations were from the ladder with someone putting a decent amount of weight on it."

Max and Mia absorbed the information, and Mia wrote again on her notepad. Granny couldn't help but to glance down at her appearance. She pursed her lips and said, "I don't weigh that much Morris," with a touch of indignation.

She turned to the side and looked into the glass of the curio cabinet. "It's these bulky shoes." Before anyone could comment Morris' voice rang out of the watch phone.

"Here we go. The results are in. What we're looking at is a bit of dried grass, Bermuda grass, to be specific. It's a very common grass and used rather extensively by many golf courses in Florida. Stuck to the larger bit was a millimeter-long tip of Tiff Eagle, which is sometimes used for the tee. Each golf course is different. Let me run the data against the golf . . . courses that are locally to you . . . and we'll see which ones use that mix."

After several minutes of silence Morris continued, "Ah, here it is. This particular blend is used by the Sunny Hill Country Club and it's just thirty minutes from you."

Mr. Delacomb gasped loudly.

"What is it Mr. Delacomb?" asked Granny.

"I know that country club. My wife's in a golf league there."

Max and Mia glanced at each other.

"Mr. Delacomb," Granny said gently, "your wife is now a suspect. We'll need to speak with her as soon as possible."

"She's gone shopping but will return later. You can speak with her then," answered Mr. Delacomb abruptly.

"Thanks Morris, we will keep you posted," said Max.

"You're welcome," said Morris's cheerful voice, all signs of annoyance gone.

Max raised his hand to his chin and paced the room, thinking about the information he had just heard. His short walk took him to the window where he saw the side edge of a large white shed.

"Mr. Delacomb, you said that you had a landscaper?"

Mr. Delacomb said, "Yes, that's right. Tom Kemper comes twice a week. He mows the lawns, keeps the shrubbery in check, maintains the gardens. I met him . . . at the Sunny Hill Country Club. He's the head greens keeper there. He's always done a very nice job maintaining the fairways and putting greens, so I asked him to work my property as well. But I don't understand why—"

"Because, I highly doubt that your wife would have blades of grass on her clothing. Shoes maybe if she walked through a newly cut lawn, but to get this bit of grass into the cabinet, one had to have the grass clipping on a sleeve. A landscaper might, especially if he went from one job to the other."

"And how does that help us find the glasses?" asked Mr. Delacomb.

"The cryptogram said to meet on sixteen at noon. Sixteen, not the sixteenth, as if it were a date. The thief means for us to meet on the sixteenth hole, and probably at the Sunny Hill Country Club. It is only ten now, but I suggest we check out the Sunny Hill Country Club.

"But, I still don't understand," said Mr. Delacomb. "How could the thief know we'd even find his cryptogram key today? Did he mean two days ago when the glasses and sock were taken?"

"Oh, no," said Max. "He meant today . . . or, more specifically, whatever day we found the key and decoded his cryptogram."

"So, he's been sitting around the country club waiting for us to show up?"

"I seriously doubt it. However, I suspect what we'll find is not the thief, but another clue. Still we have to find that next clue to move forward. But first let's check out the shed and see what we can find. I have a feeling there's considerably more here that we're not seeing."

SIX

Everyone readily agreed. In a hurry to be off, Max quickly labeled the evidence and bagged it, while Mia tucked the cryptogram and the key into her pocket. In a moment, they had packed up the laptop and the other equipment. Mr. Delacomb had tucked the letter box into his desk drawer and locked it and the curios cabinet

It took ten minutes to take the long walk through the backyard to the shed. Mr. Delacomb slid back the door. The lawn mower—a shiny new green machine nearly the size of a small farm tractor—was sitting in front and was in impeccable condition. It hardly looked used and seemed to have been wiped down and cleaned very carefully.

"So Mr. Kemper doesn't use your mower?" asked Max.

Mr. Delacomb said, "Oh, yes, he most certainly does. But I'm most precise about the care of my equipment. I refuse to have grass clippings everywhere. He's to routinely clean and maintain all machines used on the property. He doesn't really need telling, however. One of the reasons I selected Tom was his care of the country club's equipment. I'd see those mowers and wagons—always well maintained and clean. Everyone there's been pleased with his performance. So much so that I'm not the only private party he works for."

Max glanced down at the grass they had just walked on and noticed a tinge of blue. Mr. Delacomb's grass was different from the varieties they had found in the love-letter box and the cabinet.

Max stared at the lawn mower and noticed how the seat was moved all the way to the front. "Mr. Kemper must be a short man," he observed.

"Quite the contrary," said Mr. Delacomb, "He's a particularly tall and angular sort of fellow. Likes to wear straw hats to keep the sun out of his eyes."

Max walked around the shed, admiring how each tool had its marked place, and everything was polished, almost new looking. As he stepped around the tractor, he tripped on something. Lying right next to the lawn mower was a piece of folded paper and what looked like some cereal.

"Do you recognize this cereal, Mr. Delacomb?" he asked. As Mr. Delacomb came around the tractor, Morris's voice said, "You could have asked me. It's Rainbow-O's, of course. I'd recognize that lovely cereal anywhere. One of my favorites."

Max looked to Mr. Delacomb, who nodded.

"And what is cereal doing out here in the shed?" he asked.

Mr. Delacomb shrugged. "It's a favorite cereal around here, as well. My wife and son love it. Every morning for breakfast—or nearly so—and they both munch it in front of the TV at night, especially if they're watching *National Treasure*—it's their favorite movie. They've seen it, oh, dozens of times."

Mia made some notes on her notepad again while Max opened the paper he had picked up and read it. It was a cryptogram. He handed it to his sister. "Mia, it is another cryptogram. Can you solve this please?" asked Max.

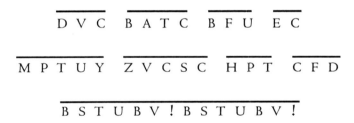

D V C   B A T C   B F U   E C

M P T U Y   Z V C S C   H P T   C F D

B S T U B V ! B S T U B V !

Mia exchanged her notepad for the cryptogram key and went to work. After several minutes of double checking her work, she read aloud her results.

"_____
_____"

(CAN YOU DECODE THIS CRYPTOGRAM, TOO?)

"What on earth does it mean?" said Mr. Delacomb. "That could be anywhere! A restaurant, a table somewhere, a—"

"The kitchen!" said Granny smoothly.

"That's my guess as well," Max said, smiling. "Let's not make this more complicated than it is. The trail of Rainbow-O's cereal clearly points to the house. They're at least a few days old too because ants are all over them."

"I didn't notice," said Mr. Delacomb feeling a bit dense, but then the expression on his face changed.

Max noticed his concerned look, but didn't ask him about it just then. "I suspect this trail of cereal was also a clue, and not just left here on accident. What do you think, Mr. Delacomb?" asked Max.

Mr. Delacomb closed his eyes briefly and took a deep breath. "My wife and son love Rainbow-O's cereal. They often snack on it. I have at times found trails of it around the house. I'd hate to think—"

"Do you eat Rainbow-O's cereal?" asked Mia.

"No!" answered Mr. Delacomb quickly. "Cold cereal upsets my stomach first thing in the morning, and I find it too sweet for a snack. I much prefer pancakes in the morning. My wife thinks that way too fattening but my son often joins me."

Mia quickly pulled out her notepad, scribbling ferociously as her hand moved left to right.

"Does your wife garden?" asked Max.

"Why, yes, she has a lovely water garden on the other side of the house. Believe it or not, it is something she truly enjoys. She says that it is relaxing. I've seen her in this shed many times. Her tools are over there."

Everyone turned and saw a large bag of dirt with pink flowered gloves lying across it. Next to that was several small hand tools sitting on top of a small bench used to kneel on when gardening and knee pads, but there was something else that caught their eye—inside a small gardening cart that held a trowel and hoe was a small empty snack box of Rainbow-O's.

"Does your wife always keep food in here Mr. Delacomb?" asked Granny.

"Well, rodents would be into it too easily, but she had a case of those snack-box-size packages of Rainbow-O's in the pantry next to the kitchen. She likes bringing a box with her when she gardens because she often misses lunch when she's deeply involved with her flowers. As I said before, she loves to eat them." Mr. Delacomb thought for a moment, then said sadly, "All these clues lead to her don't they? I'm beginning to believe there's a good chance my dear wife stole her own birthday present." He sat down on a bench and rested his forehead in his hand.

Max and Mia glanced at each other with concern. Max was about to voice his opinion but decided against, his attention now focusing on the floor. Mia opened her mouth to say something, but quickly shut it.

Granny, however, was not one to beat around the bush. She patted the man's shoulder and smiled gently at Mr. Delacomb. "Yes they do," she said in a comforting tone, "and yet she may also have absolutely nothing to do with it. Unfortunately, it goes the same for your maintenance man. All evidence so far has been entirely circumstantial. It's hard to know what's real and what just happens to be at the wrong place at the wrong time."

Granny glanced briefly at Max and Mia and smiled, nodding her head. "But what we know for sure is that we need to follow the trail of clues we've been given and see where it leads. My guess is that we need to see your kitchen."

Mr. Delacomb nodded and stood up, looking downcast but resolute. After everyone exited, he closed the shed, and they all trooped off towards the house. As they were walking Max noticed small holes along the trail. These were particularly interesting as they were like little circles with one flattened side, almost half-moons. He nudged Mia and pointed them out. While the small holes started toward the house along the same way they were going, they soon veered off to the right and ended when they came to a brick patio. Mia drew a picture of the shape and made a note on her notepad as they crossed the lawn to the kitchen entrance, which had its own small porch and a sliding glass door.

As they stood in the kitchen staring at a very clean, large, almost industrial space where Max suspected the housekeeper ruled, Max asked, "Where do you keep your Rainbow-O's cereal, Mr. Delacomb?"

Mr. Delacomb stepped over to a walk-in pantry, one whole shelf of which held various sizes and flavors of the family's favorite cereal.

"Oh my!" commented Mia as she stepped forward to assess the boxes. She made notes of the varieties and quantity of the cereal.

Max had other concerns. He studied the boxes for several seconds, then stepped forward and pulled one out. "This one," he said. "Let's look inside this one."

"Why would you want to—" began a surprised Mr. Delacomb, but he didn't object as Max carried the box to the table. With interest, he watched as Max studied the box, turning it over and over before carefully prying at what looked like a factory-sealed top. To his and everyone else's great surprise, when the flap was opened, they discovered a key taped to it. It was a small metal key uniquely shaped with a very short handle and was the size of a half-dollar.

"How did you know to open this box?" asked Mr. Delacomb as he stared at Max in amazement.

"Deduction, my dear man. If you glance at the cereal boxes, you will notice that they are all facing the same way and are lined up by color—except for this one," said Max as he placed his hand on the box. "This box was turned around and upside down. It was the only box out of order, which means that the person who put it there was perhaps in a great hurry or had other pressing concerns." Max motioned for Mia to dust the box for prints, but again there was nothing. He then detached the key from the box, raising it up for all to see.

"Mr. Delacomb, does this key belong to anything that you might own?" asked Granny.

Mr. Delacomb reached out for the key and turned it over and over in his hand, studying it carefully. Not recognizing it, he shook his head. "I can't say I've ever seen a key like this. It certainly doesn't belong to me." He returned the key to Max.

"Well, sir, if you don't mind, I'll just hold onto this for the time being. I feel we may have need of it but I can only think of one place to put it for safe keeping."

"Indeed," said Granny. "Mia?"

Max turned toward his sister, already having an idea what Granny was going to suggest.

"Can you please put the key in your pocket?" Granny said to Mia. "I know it'll be safe with you."

Mia took the key and placed it into her pocket proudly. Max smiled at his sister before glancing at his watch. "I believe we should be heading to Sunny Hill Country Club, don't you Mr. Delacomb?" Mr. Delacomb glanced at his watch and nodded. It was eleven o'clock. Max and Mia followed Granny and Mr. Delacomb through the kitchen and down a long wood-paneled hallway toward the front door.

SEVEN

THE SUNNY HILL COUNTRY CLUB was only thirty minutes from Mr. Delacomb's estate. The golf course was particularly well-maintained, with well-trimmed, lush grass and fairways that were nicely landscaped and well-watered. When they arrived, the limo driver pulled up to the entrance of the clubhouse. It didn't take long for a young man, dressed in the green and yellow colors that represented the golf course, to open the car door and offer them assistance.

"Can I help you with your golf bags, sir?" asked the boy politely. He had short, blond hair and a nice smile. His shirt was neatly pressed and tucked securely into the waist of his pants.

"No, that won't be necessary," replied Mr. Delacomb. "We can handle the bags ourselves, but we would like a golf cart if you wouldn't mind."

"Of course, sir," answered the boy, "right away!"

The boy then took off around the side of the building to fetch a golf cart. Mr. Delacomb popped the trunk, and Max grabbed his equipment bag and set it onto the pavement by his feet. Granny stood on the walk looking at the clubhouse, while Mia studied the nearby flags for an idea of where the sixteenth hole was located.

"Why don't the three of you go ahead without me," spoke Granny abruptly. "I'm going to look for clues here at the clubhouse. I have a feeling something's being hidden from us, and whatever it is smells fishy." Granny took in several long sniffs in emphasis, then she began to smell herself. "Wait a minute—false alarm—that's just me." Granny immediately reached in her hand bag for her perfume and sprayed herself. "I'm not quite sure how I picked up that particular smell, but now I'm much better."

Max and Mia shook their heads. Sometimes they just didn't understand their grandmother. Max offered, "Are you sure about this, Granny?"

"Absolutely! Perhaps I'll have a chat with the golf instructor. I need some help hitting a driver. I haven't quite mastered the stroke yet, but eventually I will. All I need to do is keep trying, and find the guidance of a really talented golf pro. " Granny then smiled at everyone and took off, leaving the group to stare after her. At that precise moment the boy drove up with a golf cart and parked it right in front of Mr. Delacomb. The trio hopped in and drove off.

"So, what was that all about?" asked Mr. Delacomb.

"You mean Granny?" said Max. "She likes to do her own thing. She maybe wanted to get a nice cup of tea. She'll be fine."

With five minutes to spare they made their way to the sixteenth hole. When they arrived Max suggested they wait as a team of two people putted out and moved to the seventeenth hole. After waiting to see if there were any more golfers wanting to use the hole, Mr. Delacomb drove the golf cart up a slight hill to the edge of the green and stopped. Max and Mia got out. Mr. Delacomb stayed in the golf cart and waited for them, along with their equipment bag.

Max glanced at his watch as they slowly approached the pin. It was noon. They felt as if something strange was going to happen and almost retreated back to the golf cart when they saw something. Max and Mia walked closer to the pin and glanced at the flag pole. The flag was green with a white number sixteen on it. Thin and flexible to endure the wind that often blew, the pole seemed typical of others they had passed. Max took out his magnifying glass and studied the pole, but it wasn't until another gust of wind blew that he noticed something odd going on with the flag. He lifted the pole from its hole and brought the flag down to where he could study it. There was a cut in the fabric in shape of a circle. There was also a tiny metal box and string of wire.

"Now, that's different," said Max as he rubbed his chin. Mia saw the hole and smiled broadly. She then took off to fetch their equipment bag. She hastily unzipped the bag and dove her hand inside. It took only a few seconds for her to find what she was looking for. She showed her brother a golf ball.

"Max, I have a sneaky suspicion that we're going to need this." Mia stepped closer to the pin, reached up and placed the golf ball next to the hole in the flag. It looked like a perfect fit.

"I think your right, Mia. Go ahead and put the ball in the hole," said Max.

Mia tipped her fingers and the ball dropped, making a loud thud as it landed into the cup.

"Look Max, a hole-in-one," said Mia as she chuckled to herself. Suddenly, they heard a loud, "*Ting!*"

Max and Mia looked around but could not tell where the sound had come from—until they heard Mr. Delacomb yell, "Over here!" The pair hurried over to the golf cart. "Something started running in the back of the cart. I'm sure of it."

Max went around to the back of the cart and lifted the cover off the wheel compartment. A small printer was just finishing spitting out a piece of paper and turned off. Max analyzed the small printer.

"Brilliant," he said as he reached out and grabbed the paper. He glanced at it, smiled and handed the paper to Mia. "It is another cryptogram."

OM HPT APPX VFSY CUPTNV

HPT ZOAA MOUY F GVPZ

PM VOGDPSOB QSPQPSDOPUG

Mia quickly snatched the cryptogram from Max's hand while pulling the key out of her pocket. She then plopped onto the ground, laid the key out in front of her on the smooth, short grass of the green, grabbed her pen and went to work. It didn't take long until she had the cryptogram solved.

"

"

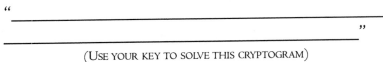

(USE YOUR KEY TO SOLVE THIS CRYPTOGRAM)

Mia read the decoded message to Max.

"What's going on?" asked Mr. Delacomb as he got out of the golf cart to see what Max and Mia were doing.

"I'm not sure," Max said with some urgency, "but we need to get out of here. People waiting on the tee to use the hole, and there's nothing more for us here." He glanced back at the man practicing his swing on the tee while a woman sat in the golf cart waiting.

"Yes, we should indeed. Come on," said Mr. Delacomb. After making sure they left nothing behind, the trio moved quickly to their golf cart, clambered aboard and drove back to the clubhouse parking lot. Max loaded their bag into the limo while Mia and Mr. Delacomb watched a young man come out of the clubhouse to return their golf cart to the side of the building. After having seen a number of the caddies and cart boys, Max realized this young man was different from the other boys they had seen earlier, different from the neat, polite boy who had greeted them. Tall and lanky, with long blond hair that seemed in need of a haircut, he kept running his hands through it trying to keep it out of his eyes. Compared to the other boys, this one seemed ill-kempt. His white tee shirt with dark round stains on the bottom peeked through underneath his green and yellow golf shirt, which also had escaped his pants.

"All finished with the golf cart sir?" the young man asked Mr. Delacomb.

"Yes, you can take it," answered Mr. Delacomb, with a wave of his hand. He handed the man both the key to the machine and a five-dollar tip.

The man pocketed the money quickly and hopped into the golf cart.

Before he left, Mia asked him, "How many greens keepers are employed here?"

The teen gave her a strange expression, but said, "One head guy and three below him."

"Is the head greens keeper about today?"

"Mr. Kemper?" the man replied.

"Yes, Mr. Kemper," replied Mia sweetly.

"He left a little while ago. His son was coming here to pick him up when his car broke down on I-75. That expressway is about twenty minutes away from here to the west."

"What does Mr. Kemper usually drive?" asked Mia.

"An old red four-by-four truck, but it's in the shop, which was why his son was going to pick him up. He left a few minutes ago with a woman in a silver Mercedes. I have no idea who she was—I haven't been working here that long—but I heard her offer to take him to his son."

Max glanced past the boy and saw a lawn mower sitting to the side of the clubhouse.

"Is that one of your lawn mowers?" asked Max.

"Yes! Mr. Kemper was in the process of fixing it when he got the call from his son. I used it to cut the fairways this morning. It worked great until I got back here. Then it started making some funny noises."

"Did he sit on the machine at all?"

"Yeah, a few times," answered the young man.

"Were you aware that Mr. Kemper works as a landscaper on the side?"

The boy smiled at Max, not at all surprised by his question. "He's got a landscaping company. Everybody wants to hire him. The golf course is all the advertising he needs. Just look what he has done around here. The man's amazing."

"He must have other people working for him. If he's the heads greens keeper of this golf course, when does he have time to do anything else?" asked Max.

"You would be surprised," answered the boy. "But, yeah, he does have a few other men working for him."

"Who are these men?" asked Mia.

"The three greens keepers that work here also work for Mr. Kemper's landscaping company. You don't get the greens and fairways looking this good without a little team work."

"I see," said Mia as Max took over the questioning.

"Are all three men working now?"

"I don't really know. I could check for you, if it's important. It'll just take a few minutes," replied the young man.

"Thank you very much for your help," said Mia.

"Not a problem," said the teen as he drove the cart away.

Max headed straight to the lawn mower. For a lawn mower that was used frequently, it was spotless. Max walked around the machine, studying it. When he glanced at the seat though, he stopped. The seat was moved towards the back of the lawn mower suggesting that Mr. Kemper was a tall man with long legs, as Mr. Delacomb had said.

Soon three tall men came around the building towards them. All wore the same colored shirts as their co-workers. Though they headed for Mr. Delacomb, Mia stepped up and proceeded to question them while Max took out a measuring tape from their equipment bag and measured each one from ankle to hip, which they tolerated, but thought was very strange. By the time they left to continue their work, Max was confused. He talked over his concerns with Mia.

"Only Mr. Kemper cut Mr. Delacomb's lawn the other day. These guys stayed here at the golf course."

"That's what they said," Mia concurred.

"But Mr. Kemper is a very tall man. Look at the distance the seat on this mower has been pushed back. Even if one of them mowed Mr. Delacomb's lawn, none of those other men would have set the seat on Mr. Delacomb's mower so far forward. They're all too tall. Everyone says Mr. Kemper was a particularly tall man, probably at least as tall as his three guys. So who drove the lawn mower at the Delacomb's estate?"

Mia shrugged. She had no idea either.

Frustrated, Max glanced toward the other side of the clubhouse. "Where did Granny go? The driving range is over there, and yet she's no where to be seen."

Mia and Mr. Delacomb also looked towards the driving range. "You know Granny. She probably wandered off somewhere," said Mia.

Max was about to raise his arm to talk into his watch phone when he heard a loud scream, and then some laughter. As the trio turned their head toward the noise, they saw Granny at the helm of a golf cart, which was swerving all over the place, even nearly dancing on two wheels. Granny had a wide smile on her face as she zigzagged the cart toward them, driving with one hand while she held a pink golf ball in the other, waving it for all to see. In her excitement she almost lost control of the golf cart, narrowly missing a tree, hopping a curb, then scooting between two parked cars. Max, Mia, and Mr. Delacomb all cringed at the accumulation of near misses.

When the golf cart screeched to a stop in front of them, Granny jumped out, still waving the golf ball.

"Look what I found! Can you believe it? A pink golf ball! I thought they only came in white."

Max and Mia shook their heads at their eccentric Granny. She was amused by the simplest of things.

"Where did you go?" asked Mia.

"After I practiced my swing with the golf pro— and, boy, was he cute," commented Granny as she waved her hand in front of her face, "I went to find you guys, but you'd already left the sixteenth hole. So, I drove my golf cart around the edge of the green and turned around, but that was when I saw this pink golf ball. It was just lying on the other side of the green, can you believe it? Someone must have left it, because there was no one around when I picked it up."

"I didn't know you could drive Granny," said Max.

"Just because I don't have a car doesn't mean that I don't know how to drive, Maxwell," answered Granny.

"I'm actually surprised that they gave you a golf cart," added Mia.

"Well—technically—they didn't. I was looking around the golf carts for clues and just decided to drive one. You know, I've never driven a golf cart before."

Mia glanced at Max and started to laugh. Mr. Delacomb politely hid his amusement behind a cough.

"Come on, Granny, enough fun for today," said Max as he turned and walked towards the limo. Within minutes everybody was inside. As the limo pulled out from the parking lot, the four people inside quickly got quiet. Granny was looking at her pink golf ball. Max was deep in thought, trying to put information together. Mia was glancing out the window, and Mr. Delacombs forehead furrowed, a wounded expression upon his face. When Max turned towards him to speak, he noticed it.

"What's wrong, Mr. Delacomb?" he asked.

Mr. Delacomb let out a long breath. "My wife drives a silver Mercedes."

This brought Mia's head around fast. Mia and Max stared at each other, not quite sure what to say. Granny turned her head and glanced at Mr. Delacomb. "What are you talking about?"

"While you were gone, we found out that Mr. Kemper had left with a woman in a silver Mercedes. We also had the opportunity to question the men who work for his landscaping company, and they said he was the one who had last used Delacomb's lawn mower, and yet the evidence proves otherwise. What we really need is to find Mr. Kemper and find out the truth."

EIGHT

FRUSTRATED AGAIN MAX STARED out the window. After several minutes, Max glanced at Granny. She was holding the pink golf ball, admiring it, when he saw some writing on it. He leaned forward and stared at the writing. He might have expected the name of the company that manufactured the ball to be printed on it, but what he saw was something hand penned onto the ball. Max read the word "Museum" written on it.

Amazed, Max sat staring for several seconds, almost breathless. "You know, Granny, have I told you how much I loved you today?"

"I love you too, Max," replied Granny.

"Good, I'm glad to hear it, because I just solved the meaning of the last cryptogram. Take a look at your golf ball." Everyone's attention now focused on the golf ball. Granny read the word aloud. "Museum! Why would someone write that on my golf ball."

"We were supposed to find that particular golf ball. It's a clue left by the thief. Remember what the cryptogram said? It said a show of historic proportions," said Max.

"Yes, and a museum is one place filled with history," added Mia.

"You got it!" Max pointed at his sister and smiled as he raised his left arm so he could speak into his watch phone. "Morris!"

Within seconds, Morris' voice could be heard. "Yes, Max!"

"Is there a museum nearby?" asked Max.

"Already checking. According to your GPS, you're not too far from . . ." Morris' voice trailed off, but they could easily hear the rapid tapping of keys as his fingers typed at lightening speed. "Aha! Found it. The Collier County Museum is located five minutes east of downtown

 Naples at the Government Center. It's about twenty-five minutes from where you are. There are several exhibits going on now. The museum usually focuses on country and Florida-state history, but one of today's exhibits focuses on . . . wait for it . . . Famous Glasses in History, mainly from important people who lived in Florida." Mia, Max, Granny, and Mr. Delacomb all stared at each other. "It also has a five-acre botanical park with a native plant garden and orchid house. I'll admit that orchids are beautiful. My favorites are the purple flowers. The color some how speaks to me."

"Yeah, yeah. Thanks, Morris. I'll be getting back with you soon," said Max as he laughed, lowering his arm.

"Though I need to get this mystery solved, I'm starving. Are you all hungry?" asked Mr. Delacomb. "I know a place nearby where we can eat. It's my treat."

"That'd be nice Mr. Delacomb, thank you," said Granny.

"I didn't realize how hungry I was until now," said Mia. "My stomach's starting to growl just at the thought of something to eat." She placed her hand on her stomach in emphasis.

They stopped at a upscale restaurant. Max and Mia noticed just how upscale after they sat down at their table and glanced at the menu. One of the items they saw was a cheeseburger. There was no picture, but the description included several items they couldn't identify. The price was eighteen dollars—and that was without fries, though you could order some on the side. What did come with the cheeseburger on its toasted artisan bread was a mandarin salad with raspberry vinaigrette, walnuts, and greenery with French names that could have been oak or maple leaves, for all they knew. Mia and Max glanced at each other and shook their heads.

"Whatever happened to just old fashioned cheeseburgers," Max whispered to his sister. "You know, the ones that were made on a regular bun with beef, ketchup, cheese, lettuce, and tomato? Now we have cheeseburgers on artisan bread or a gluten-free rice-flour bun with meat, cheese, pineapple, and drizzled with some kind of fruit sauce and does that say—kiwi?"

"I just love this place," said Mr. Delacomb. "The food is simply delicious. Have you decided what you want to eat?"

Granny nodded, not at all as distressed as her grandchildren.

"You know," Max whispered behind his menu to his sister, "we've earned adult respect for the work we do in solving things. I almost get used to being treated as an adult. But when it comes to food—"

"—you're still six," finished his sister, with a giggle. "Yeah, I know. Just order the hamburger and pick off what you don't like."

"Pick off sauce?"

The waitress appeared beside the table, her pen already poised to take their order.

Trying not to laugh, Mia said politely, "Could you give us just one more minute please?"

She and Max put their heads together and searched the menu trying to find something they'd consider eating. They decided on hamburgers without the sauce, fries, and chocolate milk shakes. The waitress soon took their order but returned shortly to drop off some waters and a coffee for Mr. Delacomb.

While they waited for their food to come, the conversation focused on the case.

"The person who last drove your lawn tractor," Max said, "was not Mr. Kemper. My impression of the man, even without meeting him, is that he's hard-working, dedicated, and likely not our thief."

"But the grass you found in the curio cabinet suggests he might be."

"True," said Max, but I suspect that was planted. Let's just say too much evidence is pointing at him. The grass, the cereal in the tool shed, clues there, at the golf course and in the curio cabinet. Someone is going to great lengths to point in Mr. Kemper's direction. But what I've seen of the machines and tools he uses and his meticulous care of your property and the golf course does not suggest a man who messes up on details. Further, there were no fingerprints in any of the locations where we found cryptograms and clues. Why would someone be so careful on the one hand and so sloppy on the other?"

Mr. Delacomb nodded, not particularly happy with this information. "So, who does that leave?"

"Not that many people knew that you had purchased the glasses, and they disappeared very soon after you hid them. It feels as if the thief was probably close to you. I assume your wife is of a modest height?"

"Yes," said Mr. Delacomb. "Five-four." He said this reluctantly, almost sadly.

"And how old is your son?"

"Fifteen."

"And is he your height or . . ."

"Actually he takes after my wife's side of the family, all of whom were fairly short. He'll never be a basketball player, that's for sure, but, well, he has his gifts. I'm a hand's on kind of guy. He's all in his head. We . . . we don't always get along."

Their food arrived and, while Granny and Mr. Delacomb raved about their food and ate heartily, Max and Mia dissected their burgers before they ate them. But as they ate, they had to admit that the combination of flavors, though unusual and not familiar to their palates, did compliment one another.

When they finished, Mr. Delacomb paid the bill, leaving the waitress a nice tip. When they got into the limo, Max looked at his watch. An hour and a half had passed. Mr. Delacomb instructed his driver to head for the Collier County Museum.

The museum was a small stone building with a large red banner hanging in front touting the very unusual glasses exhibit. There were lots of people heading inside, and parking was pretty well filled near the museum. The driver suggested that he drop them off and find someplace to park the limo. They piled out and joined the crowd heading inside. Inside looked even more crowded than the outside steps. At the door, they paid the entry fee and tried to stay close to one another as they shuffled into the first large room. It took a few minutes for Max and Mia to get close enough to begin to see the exhibit. Then he grabbed her hand and began to slip between much taller bodies.

Wall to wall tables of sunglasses were either on display or for sale. Hanging from the ceiling was a large pair of fancy black sunglasses and in locked cases around the room were famous sunglasses worn by movie stars and presidents, as proven by the photographs that accompanied them.

Mr. Delacomb was quickly turned off by the crowds and opted to wait by the door, feeling a little claustrophobic. Granny decided to go into the next room to check out what was there, while Max and Mia wanted to see the complete exhibit and stayed. Max and Mia glanced at the sunglasses displayed on the tables around the room. Their eyes took in every table and every pair of sunglasses. They were half-way around the room when they spotted a pair of sunglasses sitting in a locked clear acrylic case.

Inside the case was a pair of black, diamond studded, Prada sunglasses lying on top of a decorative green sock. Mia and Max glanced at each other and then glanced around to see if they could spot Granny, but it was way too crowded, and they couldn't see her. Max leaned close to get a good look at them, practically pressing up against the acrylic case, when a man behind him spoke to the man behind the counter. "So, how much are those glasses?"

The two conversed a few moments, negotiating a price.

"Sir, you can't purchase these sunglasses," said Max.

The man behind the table glared at him, as did the customer. "What are you talking about, boy?" said the man behind the table. "I'm here to sell these sunglasses. This pair in particular was worn by Marilyn Monroe, and unless you're willing to pay more than $25,000 dollars for them, then they are sold. The sock was worn by her as well and comes with the deal."

The man was about to turn around when he heard Max say, "These sunglasses were stolen a few days ago from a nearby estate, they were made especially for my client, so no celebrity ever wore them. And if by some miracle Marilyn Monroe came back to life and decided to put them on, then I'm really a fish who lives on land and drinks root beer."

The man gave Max a strange look, not really sure on how to reply. He then spouted, "If these sunglasses were stolen, where is your proof?"

"Well, for starters, here is the proof of who I am." Max took out his wallet and showed the man his badge. "My name is Maxwell Holmes and I am a detective. These sunglasses were made especially for my client. I have photographs of them as well as documentation that will prove they were bought and paid for by my client. Do you have a receipt for their purchase?"

The man next to Max was already back-pedaling away. But the man behind the counter narrowed his eyes. "You can't be no detective. You're, what, ten maybe?"

Max sighed. "No, sir, I'm fourteen, but I am a detective with Scotland Yard."

"Like to see you prove that." He grinned.

Max leaned toward him. "Well, let's see. You're not from Florida originally. I'd say upstate New York, but you spent three years in California and just came here, probably escaping some unpleasantness with someone's wife. You've been in Florida three weeks, and have been staying in one motel after another, still a little worried about California. You made up what you've said about the sunglasses, but you know they're worth a good price and saw this exhibit as a likely venue for their sale. The sock, as far as you know, was just the conveyance for the glasses. How am I doing so far?"

As Max had been talking, the man's confident smile fell, then his mouth hung open, then he went pale. "How'd you know so much about me?"

"Any linguist could trace your mixed accent, and the rest was based on your reactions as I spoke. Those glasses are stolen property."

"Okay!" the man said. "Look, those sunglasses aren't even mine. A guy gave them to me to sell. I just get a cut. I didn't know they were stolen."

"Who gave them to you?" asked Max.

"He's around here somewhere," he said and glanced around trying to locate him.

Curious, Max glanced by the door where Mr. Delacomb was standing. He pointed. "Did that man give them to you?"

The man glanced at Mr. Delacomb. "No, that's not the guy." The man reached down, grabbed a piece of scrap paper, and quickly wrote something down, handing it to Max. "This is the man. I was just trying to do him a favor." Max glanced at the paper. The letters were out of order.

EREMPK

"You were just doing a man a favor and were going to make him $25,000 dollars."

The man shrugged his shoulders.

"And what was your cut going to be?"

"Twenty percent!"

"If you help us, I won't have you arrested, but keep in mind that I can at anytime," spoke Max.

"Understood."

Max nodded and turned away from the table speaking to Mia in hushed tones. "Do you still have the key?"

Mia placed her hand in her pocket and pulled out the small key, showing him.

"Good!" Max looked left and then right as he reached for the case with the diamond studded sunglasses. He then pulled the case to him and watched as Mia placed the key into the lock and turned it. It was a perfect fit. The lock clicked opened, but instead of opening the case and taking the sunglasses, Max merely locked it back again and told Mia to put away the key.

Max was about to turn around when a sweet smelling perfume filled the air. The scent was pleasant, and one that he immediately recognized. He quickly glanced around, trying to find the source, when he recognized someone's voice.

Max turned back towards the crowd where he glimpsed a young man with untidy hair. Recognition hit Max as he noticed the oil stain on his tee-shirt hidden underneath a blue button-down shirt. It was the teen from the golf course who had taken their golf cart and spoken with them.

Max quickly grabbed Mia's hand while he held the acrylic case tightly to his chest. He maneuvered out of the crowd and away from the table where he could tell Mia what he had seen, but when he tried to turn and move to the left, he felt Mia stop. Not prepared, he pulled Mia's arm. As he moved closer to her, his foot slid on something. Confused, Max glanced down to see what it was. There were grass clippings on the floor being scattered from the crowd. Max turned around to mention it to Mia when he noticed her staring at something. She also took an intake of breath. His eyes then followed her gaze as they saw a man talking with Mr. Delacomb wearing a red baseball cap. Mia recognized the man. The two were arguing, both becoming extremely red-faced with their anger. The siblings waited for the pair to part before walking over to Mr. Delacomb.

"Is anything wrong, Mr. Delacomb?" asked Mia.

Mr. Delacomb, still breathing hard, shook his head. He caught his breath and said, "No, not at all. Why do you ask?" spoke Mr. Delacomb calmly.

Mia was about to answer but stopped when she felt her brother squeeze her hand.

"No reason," replied Mia.

Then Mr. Delacombs eyes found the case. His eyes lit up, and he clasped his hands in joy. "You found them?" he asked excitedly. "You found my wife's sunglasses?" Mr. Delacombs eyes filled with his relief as he placed his hand to his chest, exhaling a deep breath.

"Yes, we did. The sock as well. Have you seen Granny?" asked Max, as he turned his gaze towards the table where he had found the sunglasses to see if the man from the golf course was still standing there, but he had disappeared.

"I saw her go out the door near the back of the room. I have no idea where she was going."

"Did anyone else go out that door, before or after her?" asked Mia.

Mr. Delacomb thought for a moment. "I don't think so, but I really wasn't paying much attention."

"Come on," Max said. "Let's see if we can find her. Something must have caught her attention."

The trio began to move through the crowd when a woman in a tan shirt walked up to them. "Are you Maxwell Holmes?" asked the woman.

"I am he."

"I work here at the museum. A woman gave this to me to give to you." The woman raised her hand and gave Max the letter. She then turned into the crowd and disappeared. Max opened the letter and read it, with Mia looking over his shoulder.

Max, I am following a clue. Don't worry, I'll be careful. Morris will know where to find me. Meet me later along with Mia to discuss my findings. Set up a meeting with all of the suspects for tonight. You know what to do.

Granny

"What is it?" asked Mr. Delacomb.

"We know where Granny went. She'll be meeting us back at your estate. In the meantime, we'll need to find all of the suspects and have them meet us in your library tonight at seven o'clock. By then we'll know who committed the crime."

"But who are all of the suspects?"

Max quickly wrote down some names on a piece of paper and handed it to Mr. Delacomb.

"Can you make sure that these individuals attend?" Mr. Delacomb glanced at the names.

"Absolutely, but what about this one?" said Mr. Delacomb as he pointed at one name.

"We'll take care of him. Now if you'll excuse us, we are going to check on a few things. We'll take a cab back to our hotel and meet you back at your estate this evening," said Max.

Mr. Delacomb nodded and was about to grab the case with the sunglasses, when Max held it back. "We'll hold onto the case until this evening, sir." With that said Max and Mia walked away from Mr. Delacomb, through the crowd and headed for the botanical gardens.

NINE

AT 7:00 O'CLOCK THAT evening, Max, Mia and Granny walked into Mr. Delacombs library with the sunglass case in their hands. Waiting in the room for them was Mr. Delacomb, along with his wife, who was sitting next to him filing her nails as if she were bored. His fifteen-year-old son, Robert, was sitting next to his mother in jeans and a Metalica T-shirt, his backpack on the floor next to him. Mr. Kemper, who was sitting in an opposite chair from the family, still wore his lawn mowing attire.

"I know you must all be wondering why you're here," said Max as he set the case onto the desk. The room was filled with silence as if everyone were afraid to speak. "For those of you who may not know, my name is Maxwell Holmes. This is my sister, Mia, and our Granny, Nellie Holmes. We're detectives and are here to solve the case of the missing sock. As you can see, we have successfully recovered the sock."

"This is about your disgusting old socks that *maybe* belonged to Elvis's grandmother?" said Mr.

Delacomb's wife. She formed her highly polished fingers into fists and planted them on her hips.

Mr. Delacomb turned red and squirmed in his chair. Max opened the case with the key and pulled out the sock for all to see. He handed it to Mr. Delacomb. "Perhaps it would be appropriate if you give your wife her birthday present a bit early."

"Yes," he said, eager to recover a bit of good graces. He slid out the diamond-studded sunglasses and held them out to his wife. "My dear, I truly believed that your fascination with sunglasses was a serious form of compulsive illness. You have proven me wrong. Therefore, I wish to give you this pair to ask your forgiveness and add to your collection."

The woman's eyes opened wide, and her hands went to her mouth. "Oh, Charles! Oh, they're absolutely beautiful. These will be the centerpiece of my collection. I'll treasure them always. You know, dear, there's a sunglasses exhibit going on at the museum. You won't believe it, but I went. I looked all around, and, quite frankly, there was nothing I wished to buy. I do believe I've now completed that collection and can move on to something else."

Mr. Delacomb grinned. "That's great news, dear. So, what would you like to collect now? Fine first editions? Rose varieties for your garden? Coins?"

She laughed lightly. "Oh, no, dear. Those are so mundane. Anyone can collect books and coins. I hadn't considered rose varieties, and certainly there would be many kinds and oh so many colors . . . but I'll hold off on that for now. No, I was thinking of collecting . . . poodles."

Mr. Delacomb's face looked stricken. "Stuffed poodles?" he asked hopefully.

"That's a ridiculous collection. No. I intend to collect the finest breed lines and show them. I'll win trophies and travel. It'll be fun. You'll see."

"Me? You want me to come with you?"

"Of course. We'll work together on this collection. That'll be ever so much better than collecting alone. Then you can get rid of your dirty old socks and I'll sell my sunglasses . . . all except this pair, of course."

Though Mr. Delacomb looked far from happy, he smiled and patted his wife's hand.

"I believe this is yours, Mr. Delacomb," said Max as he lifted the green sock from the table. Mr. Delacomb's son's hand had been inching across the table toward the sock. He pulled his arm back when Max picked up the sock.

"Finding the sock and the sunglasses was only part of our concern," said Max, "We also needed to solve the crime. We are prepared to do so now."

Mr. Kemper stood up. "Solve what crime? Do you believe I'd stoop to invading a client's home and steal from them?"

"No," said Max. "I don't."

"Then why am I here? I've worked hard all day, and you have me sitting around with these idiots, who, quite frankly, have way too much time on their hands and not enough to do. I mean, collecting socks . . . sunglasses . . . *poodles!* I work way too hard to think any of that funny."

"We would like to begin with you Mr. Kemper," said Mia sweetly. "So you'll soon be on your way."

Mr. Kemper was a tall, handsome man with short brown hair and a mustache. "Good," he said calmly, while Mia pulled out her notepad and opened it.

"You work at the Sunny Hill Country Club, correct?" asked Mia.

"Yes, that's right. I've been the Head Greens Keeper there for going on six years now," replied Mr. Kemper.

"And yet you're also Mr. and Mrs. Delacomb's landscaper," continued Mia.

"Yes! I have a landscaping business on the side. As you can see, maintaining other people's yards is my life, which I thoroughly enjoy. For me, it's therapeutic and relaxing. In fact, I'm the landscaper for several of the members at the golf course. They make up a majority of my clientele. The rest I have gotten by word of mouth."

"I see, but you don't cut all of the lawns yourself, do you? From what I understand you have the other greens keepers to cut the country club's grass every few days. But it's you who takes great care of everything else pertaining to the club. You do a lot, Mr. Kemper, and you work hard. It shows too because every lawn I've seen looks impeccable," said Mia. "But you have limited time working so many jobs. The one thing we're positive about Mr. Kemper, is that you're not a machine."

Mr. Kemper smiled and laughed slightly.

"Mr. Kemper," said Max, "you're here this evening mostly to clear up a misunderstanding. Yesterday, did you get a ride from someone at the club to rescue your son, whose car had broken down on the highway?"

Mr. Kemper looked startled. "How'd you know that . . . yes. Mrs. Delacomb was kind enough to give me a lift. I would have driven myself, but my truck was being serviced that day, and taxis are so expensive. It was a kindness that she offered her assistance."

"Is this true, Mrs. Delacomb?"

She shrugged. "Why, yes. I was heading out to the museum and would go right past where Tom needed to be. He's such a help in the gardens and does an absolutely perfect job on the lawns . . . well, I just couldn't see leaving him stranded, even if I had to have the car vacuumed afterwards to remove all the bits of grass."

Mr. Delacomb didn't say anything, but he looked considerably relieved by this information.

Max turned to Mr. Kemper and said, "Thank you for your time, sir. That's all we needed from you. I hope you can forgive the inconvenience."

"Sure. I'll go order invisible fencing."

"I beg your pardon," said Mr. Delacomb.

"You're getting dogs—"

"Poodles," corrected Mrs. Delacomb.

"Yes, well . . . poodles, if given the chance, will dig up the gardens, pee on the shrubs and chew up the little name tags we put by expensive plants. Invisible fencing will allow you folks to keep your poodles and have your gardens, too."

He left, and, for a long moment, the room was washed in silence.

"I don't understand," said Mr. Delacomb. "Who do you think stole the sock and glasses, then?"

Max looked a little uncomfortable. "Well, sir, we were hoping the thief would come clean on his own."

As there was only one other male in the room besides Mr. Delacomb, he turned to his son. "Robert?"

The teen turned bright red and glared at Max. "You don't know anything," he said, furious. "You're just guessing. The famous Maxwell Holmes, and the rest of the Crypto-Capers—you're all a joke!"

Max allowed himself a small, satisfied smile. "Are we now? Let's just see. What do you normally eat for breakfast?"

Robert glanced around the room in confusion and then forced a laugh. "I eat Rainbow-O's or pancakes. I much prefer the pancakes. Three of them piled high with lots of maple syrup and butter. So what?"

"What kind of career are you interested in?"

"The cereal business, of course," started Robert as he glanced at his father, "I've come up with a new kind of cereal. I call it Maple Pan Crunch. It's made of wheat flour and tastes like a pancake drizzled in maple syrup. I made a trial batch and am currently trying it out on some of my friends at school. So far it's a hit. My dad won't listen to any of my ideas, and yet he wants me to help him with the company. He wants me in marketing. I want to be in development. For the past few months, I've been coming up with new flavors of cereals to help our business grow even more. I'm good at development, great at research, but I truly suck at marketing and promotion. I have access to many people and ideas. Unlike my father, I listen to our customers' opinions."

Mr. Delacomb's face became red and he glared at his son.

"I have another new idea, but father won't hear of it," finished Robert sadly.

"Son, I do listen to your opinions," spouted Mr. Delacomb.

"If that was true you'd provide funding for my projects instead of trying to shut them down?" Robert shouted.

All eyes were on Robert and Mr. Delacomb now. Mr. Delacomb closed his eyes and shook his head.

"Mr. Delacomb?" said Granny.

He waited several seconds before he raised his head and looked at Granny.

"Robert, you need to tell your father everything."

All eyes were focused on the boy now.

"You, Bobby?" said Mr. Delacomb. "You stole the glasses?"

He gave a hoot. "You think this was about the glasses? They're worth, what, twenty-five thousand? Peanuts compared to the value of the sock."

"Well, the sock—"

"Yes, dear father, it belonged to Elvis's grand-mother. Absolutely correct. But did she buy it in Target? I don't think so. As it so happens, the sock belonged to another famous person. Elizabeth Taylor wore those green socks in *Cleopatra* in 1963. Then they disappeared from the set and haven't been seen since. It turns out that Elvis's grandmother had a schoolmate who went on to Hollywood. She never was able to act, but she was a fine seamstress. She stole the socks and sent them to her friend. Those socks, worn and dirty as they are, are worth over a quarter of a million dollars. I took one to have it evaluated. I never stole anything, father."

"But you led us on a merry chase, Robert. I don't understand."

"I gave you clues to getting your sock and glasses back. My buddy at the country club helped me."

"He's referring to the new boy at the country club we spoke to before leaving. He gave us lots of good infor-mation. But he was wearing an oil-stained t-shirt under-neath various shirts he wore today, which shows that he was in a hurry and forgot to change it. I also saw the boy at the museum this afternoon. His name is Denton Miles." Max waited for the impact of his words to set in.

"That is correct," said Robert in amazement.

"Yes," said Max. "Mr. Delacomb, from the moment you showed us the first cryptogram, we knew we were not really dealing with a theft. Thieves don't give clues to what they stole. But we suspected that something was going on here that you didn't know about. Robert tried very hard to throw off suspicion, not to make good with his theft, but to give himself time to check out the value of the sock. You thought we were following the trail of the glasses, but we never were. It was always about the sock. Robert wanted to show you his expertise in research in a way that you might actually hear him, but what he wasn't counting on was the greediness of his new friend.

"Denton sabotaged Mr. Kemper's son's car, which explains the oil stains on his shirt. He had to create a distraction to lure Mr. Kemper away from the country club, and he did it in a manner that involved Mrs. Delacomb. He also wanted to lead us astray. You see, Denton stole the sock and sunglasses from Robert, wanting the money for himself, but Robert never told him how much the sock was worth, which was wise on his part. Denton did a rough estimate on the sunglasses, not thinking twice about the sock, and thought the best place to sell them was going to be at the Collier County Museum's latest exhibit. It was a perfect opportunity for him.

"After realizing what Denton had done, Robert laid out the rest of the clues for us to find, leading us to the museum. He wanted us to help find the sunglasses and the sock. But Denton was also clever. He chose a man of questionable character to sell the sunglasses for him. Denton knew that, if the man were caught by the police, it would most likely not lead back to him. But he was wrong. Granny followed Denton from the museum—that's when she disappeared. Denton admitted that he had cut the country club's grass this morning, which explains the grass pieces we found scattered on the floor of the museum, but the pieces of grass in the study came from Robert. He'd taken a joy ride on the lawn mower around the yard before he went into the study and—borrowed—the sock. If anyone wants to check my theory, we can do so at this time by having him sit on the lawn mower. I guarantee that the seat will be positioned in the correct place for him and not Mr. Kemper."

All eyes were focused on Max.

"Where is Denton now?" asked Mr. Delacomb.

"He's currently residing in the capable hands of the Las Vegas Police Department."

"Las Vegas?" said Mr. Delacomb, surprised. "He almost got away, then."

"He'd like to think so," Max said with a smile. "No, we had him the whole time. He just didn't know it."

Robert clapped his hands and shook his head. "I'm truly impressed." He then turned towards his father, his features more serious. "My innocent intentions of trying to impress you were marred by a real theft. I was at the museum trying to get the sunglasses back before you saw them. I ran into Denton, but he ran away from me. I went to go another way, but ran into you. We then proceeded to argue about why I was there, and I couldn't tell you the truth. I knew that instead of being impressed with what I had tried to do, that you would just be disappointed. I knew that you wouldn't have listened to my side. You never listen to me, even when I am trying so hard to help you." Robert paused, "Well, at least you have your precious sock and sunglasses back."

Mr. Delacomb turned to his son, tears in his eyes. "I'm so sorry, Bobby," said Mr. Delacomb. "You're so young. I never thought you'd be this interested in cereal before college. And to think you did all the research on the sock for me. I promise to listen from this moment forward."

Granny said, "We did enjoy your cryptograms, Robert, and we had fun solving this case."

Mia and Max then approached Robert. Mia handed him a folded piece of paper. "This is for you."

Robert glanced at the piece of paper and then opened it. It was a cryptogram.

"I think you'll have lots of time to figure this out before you take the reins of your father's company."

Mr. Delacomb, his voice soft with emotion, said, "I didn't believe I could hope for a good outcome in this case. I thought I had lost the glasses, thought I had lost my wife, and had no idea how to communicate with my son. You not only gave me back my property, but you made me appreciate what I had . . . and here I don't mean the sock. I have a wonderful wife, whose generous nature and quirky habits will keep me happy and entertained the rest of my life. I also have a son who I now trust will make sure I don't make a fool of myself in my own quirky habits, a young man with gifts I never learned to appreciate. And all I thought I had lost was some glasses and an old sock. I was about to lose so much more. But you found everything, restored everything to me. I will be eternally grateful.

Mr. Delacomb paid the Crypto-Capers their handsome fee plus a very generous bonus and sent them on their way home by private jet. And, thus, the case of the missing sock was added to list the crime fighters had successfully solved.

Use the key and solve the cryptogram that the Crypto-Capers gave to Robert.

KEY:

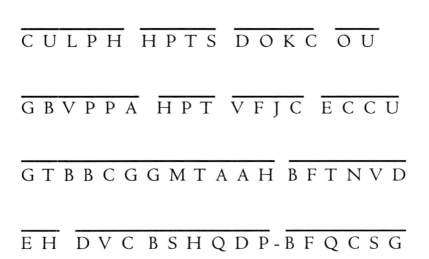

A	B	C	D	E	F	G	H	I	J	K	L	M	N	O	P	Q	R	S	T	U	V	W	X	Y	Z
F	E	B	Y	C	M	N	V	O	L	X	A	K	U	P	Q	I	S	G	D	T	J	Z	R	H	W

MESSAGE:

C U L P H   H P T S   D O K C   O U

G B V P P A   H P T   V F J C   E C C U

G T B B C G G M T A A H   B F T N V D

E H   D V C   B S H Q D P - B F Q C S G

EPILOGUE

"YOUR FLIGHT WENT WELL, THEN?" asked Morris, as he, Max and Mia sat on the sofa in the house on Baker Street, discussing the case.

"It was excellent," said Mia as she covered her eyes with her arm, wanting to take a nap.

"Was Mr. Delacomb pleased with the results of the case?"

"Oh, yes! He was so pleased in fact that we received a large bonus," said Max as he stretched. "We deposited the money into our account on the way home. Now we can afford all the new gadgets and upgrades that I'm sure you added while we were away."

Morris smiled sheepishly and was about to comment, when a bell went off on his computer.

"What in the world is that?" asked Max as he covered his ears.

"It is my World News Detector. Whenever there's something important going on in the world and our services might be needed, it goes off, informing us to check it. It's one of those things I added. It should give us a heads-up on cases so we can prepare. I also created an e-mail link for us. Look, someone's sending a message now."

Max, Morris, and Mia all rose from the sofa and moved towards the computer. As they leaned forward they noticed that the message was in a type of word scramble. Mia sat down at the desk and immediately went to work, writing down the letters on a piece of paper. The message was only a few words long. Mia scribbled feverishly trying to move around the letters to make sense. After several minutes, she turned around, holding the pieces of paper in her hand as if it were a trophy.

On the paper were these letters:

ETH EACS OF DER KORC YNCOAN

"What does it mean?" asked Morris.

She smiled. "Boys, I believe we have our next case. We're going to Las Vegas."

THE END

ANSWERS TO THE CRYPTOGRAMS

KEY

A	B	C	D	E	F	G	H	I	J	K	L	M	N	O	P	Q	R	S	T	U	V	W	X	Y	Z
F	E	B	Y	C	M	N	V	O	L	X	A	K	U	P	Q	I	S	G	D	T	J	Z	R	H	W

Page 24:
> MEET ME ON 16 AT NOON TODAY!

Page 56:
> THE CLUE CAN BE FOUND WHERE YOU
> EAT—CRUNCH! CRUNCH!

Page 67:
> IF YOU LOOK HARD ENOUGH YOU WILL
> FIND A SHOW OF HISTORIC PROPORTIONS!

Page 84:
> KEMPER

Page 101:
> ENJOY YOUR TIME IN SCHOOL!
> YOU HAVE BEEN SUCCESSFULLY CAUGHT BY
> THE CRYPTO-CAPERS.

Page 103:
> THE CASE OF RED ROCK CANYON